also by Jim Provenzano

Finding Fire
Now I'm Here
Forty Wild Crushes, stories
Message of Love
Every Time I Think of You
Cyclizen
Monkey Suit
PINS, the stage adaptation
PINS

Audiobook adaptations:

PINS (narrated by Paul Fleschner)
Every Time I Think of You (narrated by Deborah Wetherby)
Message of Love (narrated by Michael Whitacre)

The Lost Art of New York, by John Whyte, Jr.
(editor, Publisher)

also by Jim Provenzano

Finding Tulsa
Now I'm Here
Forty Wild Crushes: stories
Message of Love
Every Time I Think of You
Cyclizen
Monkey Suits
PINS the stage adaptation
PINS

Audiobook adaptations:

PINS (narrated by Paul Fleschner)
Every Time I Think of You (narrated by Michael Wetherbee)
Message of Love (narrated by Michael Wetherbee)

The Lost of New York, by John Rigney Jr.
(Editor, Publisher)

Lessons in Teenage Biology

a novella

Jim Provenzano

Myrmidude Press

copyright © 2024 Jim Provenzano.

All rights reserved. Except for brief passages, no part of this book may be reproduced, stored in or introduced into a retrieval system, or transmitted in any form without the prior written permission of the copyright owner.

Cover illustration: Plebo Industries
Cover design: Max Leger
Published by Myrmidude Press

Provenzano, Jim 1961– Lessons in Teenage Biology / Jim Provenzano

ISBN print: 979-8-218-35678-1
Ebook: 979-8-218-35680-4

1. Fiction 2. Gay Fiction 3. Literary Fiction 4. 1970s 5. Ohio 6. Coming of Age 7. Sexuality 10. Homosexuality I1. Provenzano, Jim

> "When you're seventeen,
> everything feels like the end of the world.
> Or the beginning of the world.
> And that's an awesome thing."

— Becky Albertalli, *The Upside of Unrequited*

for Mitch Walker

1. Mitochondria

A lot can happen in two days, even if you're an unremarkable closeted gay kid in a small Ohio town. But if I'd known what was going to happen, I might have stayed in bed, except for the good part that made it all worth it.

It all started as usual for a Friday morning.

"C'mon, Tom. Let's go." Dad poked his head in the bathroom door.

"Awrighff," I mumbled, brushing my teeth. I had to put my shoes on. After finishing in the bathroom, I'd be ready to go to school, with Dad and my little brother Angelo waiting in the hall.

Damn. Another day getting to school early. If Darin was late like he usually was, I'd have to be alone in the auditorium until the bell for first period. When it got cold outside, everybody had to hang out there. They all had their own crowd of friends.

I didn't. I had Darin Shortell, who wasn't even my best friend. I'd just known him all my life. He used to live next door. But his family moved out to a big ranch house off Route 42. He was usually late, so

1

I got to sit alone like a dweeb. I used to walk to school, but I'd end up being late, stopping to pet dogs and look at buildings. On good days, I'd get to school just in time to go to my locker. The first period bell would ring the moment I'd get to class. But that didn't happen very often.

I finally got ready, put on my jacket, picked up my books, and got in the car with my little brother Angelo. Dad started to pull out of the driveway. Then he stopped the car with a jolt. I turned to see Rex Hahn, my sister's boyfriend, pop his head out the window of his Camaro. He'd pulled up behind us in the driveway.

"Sorry about that, Mr. Mollicelli."

Dad got out of the car and stood in the driveway. "Good morning, Rex." Dad looked at him as if he were a dumb puppy.

"Uh, is Tara ready?" Rex tapped his hand on his side mirror. He'd been dating my sister since early summer and picked her up every morning for school and for their dates. He was a cool guy for a basketball jock, and nice to me, always greeting me in the halls at school with a low-five. A few times over summer break, he'd patiently tried to teach me how to play, but I could barely manage to dribble the ball.

He'd even agreed to run for Homecoming with Tara, and although they didn't win, he's beamed while standing with her on the crepe paper-decorated flatbed truck at the football game last month. Tara liked him a lot, I guess. She called him "obedient."

"I don't know, Rex. Why don't you just pull out and park your car and then go up to the door and find out?"

Dad said it very calmly, like if he didn't talk slow, Rex wouldn't understand him. Dad was being polite, but underneath it he was pissed. I knew.

The two of them got back in their cars, Rex backing up. Angelo and I grinned at each other.

The moment we got out of the driveway, Dad turned on the radio. One of my rock stations blared out Heart's "Barracuda," which made me feel better for a moment, but Dad turned it to his easy listening station. I hate that stuff. It's like being on Quaaludes, or at least what I think it's like, since I've never done them.

"Turn the radio off when you park the car, Tom," Dad said.

"Right." The night before, I'd taken Dad's car for a lengthy spin while picking up some groceries for Mom, blasting the radio.

"Right," Angelo echoed from the back seat.

"Shut up." I turned to fake-punch him. "Nobody's talkin' to you."

"Daaad!"

"Boys, it's not even nine o'clock yet," Dad sighed, as if there were only certain hours to hate your brother.

We sat silently as Dad drove. I leaned my head back and watched the reflections of trees go one way in the windshield while the real trees went the other way. I had every corner memorized but pretended I was on a long journey through Europe. The trip would take months, and I was headed to a remote castle where I would meet a dashing and reclusive prince, exiled because he would not marry. He would greet me at his immense castle door, where he'd invite me to meet him for dinner. We would eat at opposite ends of a twenty-foot oak table. With dinner, we'd have wine poured into hand-blown glasses–

"Get out." Angelo stood by my door, impatiently holding it open. Behind him loomed Plainfield High School. He wanted his turn in the front seat for Dad to escort him to the elementary school. He was in sixth grade. Big cheese at Taft Elementary. But I was a junior at Plainfield, Class of '78, that is, if I live another two years.

"C'mon," Angelo whined. I looked at him as if it was his fault I had to go to this crummy school. I got out. He hopped in to replace me. Off they went, Angelo to happy elementary school with crackers and crayons, king of the heap, and Dad to his terrific job at the construction company, leaving me somewhere in between. I turned and faced the old three-story brick building. The long windows yawned as the door sucked in kids. I went in, drawn like a zombie.

Fortunately, Darin Shortell was in the auditorium when I got there. I sat down beside him, barely glancing up at the noisy cluster of kids all around.

"Aurgh."

"Oooh, you're in a good mood," Darin commented.

"It's a beautiful day in the neighborhood."

I leaned my head back and looked up at the crusty auditorium ceiling. Big brown leak stains splotched up the plaster. Darin and I jokingly called these the fart stains. We imagined that if farts had colors, all the ceilings in the world would have these stains on them from people sitting below.

Darin and I were always making up gross stuff like that, which was pretty easy in a cruddy place like Plainfield High School. The building's about a hundred years old. It used to be an opera house but in the 1920s, they built classrooms around it. Every year the school board kept threatening to tear it down and build a new one, except there was never enough money passed on school bonds.

There was something about mils, too, not like mills with a cute water wheel, but a millionth of a penny. Every year *The Plainfield Journal* printed flow charts and pie charts at election time, but it got turned down every year. The real reason was that our town was full of a lot of old people who were gonna die and didn't care about kids my age. They threw all their money at the churches. There was always money to build another church in Plainfield.

I used to think it was neat having lots of churches, because the architecture of the old ones is great. But then I realized there was only one Catholic church, which was my favorite, since we used to be Catholic. There was no synagogue; only two Jewish families in Plainfield. All the rest of the churches were Christian, but with different names, like different brands of corn flakes with the same garbage on the inside.

I tried going to a Lutheran church a few times with Randy, who I'll talk about later. Randy wasn't a Born Again, he'd just been going with his parents since he was a kid and never stopped. I went more for Randy than for God. It was nice to stand next to him and sing hymns, like I did in choir.

Darin said something.

"What?" I asked.

"I said, we got a new student teacher in gym class," Darin repeated.

"What's his name?"

"I forget."

"Whadja do yesterday?"

"Basketball."

"Aw, crap."

I hated basketball. It was so complicated. Andy Krebs shouting, "Guard your man, Mollicelli! Guard your man!" I didn't know who the heck my man was. Gym class. Hell on earth, followed by a bunch of naked guys as a secret thrill.

I leaned back and stared up at the fart stains and the dusty chandelier that hung in the center of the auditorium. Most of the little light bulbs had burned out, small pointed ones made to look like real flames. I looked around the auditorium at all the kids waiting for school to start. I imagined a crowd of people with bustles and corsets and top hats dressed up to see some opera or vaudeville show. Somebody yelled up on the stage, and I flipped back to the kids.

See, the stage was also the gym, and in the morning before classes started or at lunch you either sat in the auditorium or went up to the stage/gym to play sports, which was usually battle ball, a real stupid game also known as Smear the Queer. There are two sides, and each side just throws a bunch of balls like basketballs, only lighter. If you get hit, you're out. The side that creams the other side wins. Real sophisticated, right?

Darin and I never played battle ball in the morning or at lunch. We had to play it in gym class sometimes, though, like when Mr. Geissler, the gym teacher, couldn't think of anything better to do, which was quite often. I got very nervous on gym days. With Darin having it the day before me, and always telling me, warning me, it had a more ominous threat.

Sharing our fears and dreads included knowing each other was gay, but we weren't into each other, or I wasn't. That was something we never discussed. We just knew.

The bell for first period rang. The whole auditorium rumbled with all the kids moving and kicking chairs. The kids up on the gym floor dropped the balls and headed out. I couldn't understand why those bozos liked getting all sweaty and messed up before school started. They were either jocks who had gym first period or the stoners who were always a mess. I could sometimes smell them when they walked by.

Wait, that's a jerky thing to say, since I'd smoked pot, just not all the time.

Darin took a left at the auditorium door as I headed right.

"Wait!" he called out.

"What?"

"Your flashcards."

Darin dug in his backpack for a small stack of index cards held together by a thick rubber band. We had Biology last period and I was doing okay, but I wanted an A. All the terms blurred together in my mind, so Darin thought to make flash cards, which we'd quizzed each other on at lunch the day before.

What I couldn't tell him was that I had a crush on our teacher, Mr. Hirsch. It should have motivated me, but I kept getting distracted by his tall handsome looks, his bushy mustache, and the way he filled out a pair of green corduroys. I could get an A+ on a quiz about which pants he wore to school each day.

"Thanks," I smiled and took the cards.

"Go over them at lunch."

We unfortunately had been assigned different sections of students grouped into the small cafeteria. Darin had been my lunch buddy for years. I kind of missed him.

I walked over to English in Room 101. I thought about going over to my locker since it was on the way, just to waste time, but I had all my stuff and my coat put away. I only carried my books for the morning. I changed them at lunch. It'd look dorky to carry all my books for the whole day.

Besides, if I dropped them, some joker would come along and kick them down the hall. I made sure I had all my stuff, relieved I'd gotten to school early enough, just in case my locker didn't open. I don't know what I'd do if my locker didn't open. You can't go up to a teacher and ask them to help you. Do that, and you'll look like a total jerkface. I used to have nightmares that there was a fire in school and everybody had to get their coats, but I couldn't remember my locker combination. It was so dumb. I was more scared of being laughed at than burning to death.

I was thinking of this stupid nightmare and fidgeting with my shirt-tail which kept wanting to come out, when a big herd of guys came down the hall, laughing and talking. Right in front was Brian Leonard, who was co-captain of the football team, who was not a friend, so of course he didn't say Hi to me, even though we were in Biology and Gym together.

The rest of his new friends were all football players. Brad Hawkins was one of them. I started to say hi to him, since I'd known him as long as I knew Darin. We three used to play together all the time. But he was with his football buddies and got real stuck up and pretended not to see me.

Flushing with embarrassment, it made me so mad, because Brad would only do that when he was around his jock friends. I remember in junior high the day we drifted apart; well, not drifted, more abruptly closed the book on each other.

Brad asked me if I was going out for football, and when I said, "Of course not!" real sarcastic, he looked at me like I was a Martian. I was scrawny then, and I'm still only five-foot-five. Besides, the only thing I knew about football were a few NFL team colors from games my dad watched on TV, and that a few quarterbacks were really handsome. Our family went to home games, but more to watch Tara's cheerleading.

After I told him I wasn't into football, Brad Hawkins didn't come over much after that.

Back when we were in elementary school, Brad went to St. Lawrence and didn't play with the other Catholic kids from his school. They were either too young or lived too far away. Every day I'd wait for Brad to come walking up the street in his black pants, white shirt, and black tie. I'd go upstairs with him while he changed his clothes.

One time, he was standing in his underpants and told me to take my pants off, too. I was happy and nervous and tried to pull my pants down over my shoes. They got stuck and I fell to the floor. Brad sat down next to me. "Lemme see your dick," he said. We both pulled down our shorts and started playing around until his mom called us downstairs. We rushed to get dressed.

"Don't tell anyone," Brad muttered as we sat in his kitchen drinking chocolate milk his mom made for us. We also ate Fritos, which I said looked like little bobsleds. We slid them through the air and into each other's mouths, which was kind of sexy.

So, I felt really weird having done all that stuff with Brad and him being stuck up just because he was on the football team. He walked by with all the other jocks who ignored me. It was like we broke up, even though we never really dated.

I also stopped eating Fritos.

2. Chromatid

On time for English, I sat down at my desk in Mrs. Finch's room and immediately started doodling on the cover of my notebook. I always draw. My notebooks are filled with stuff, mostly cartoons, dragons, and funny animals.

Once in a while I'd draw a real muscled guy, totally pumped, which was okay as long as it was like Frank Frazetta or those guys in *Heavy Metal*. Sometimes I'd draw them naked with big hard boners, but then I'd cover up their gonads with dark loincloths. I put big swords in their hands to fight giant serpents that slithered up from behind them. When I got bored, like in study hall, I'd fill in all the scales one by one, then smudge them to shade the serpent bodies.

Sue Shumaker, who sat in front of me, peeked over my desk while I did some smudging. She was really nice, except her voice was kind of high and too sweet. Other than that, she was okay, not totally popular, since she lived way out on Route 260 on a farm. She never stuck around for the social stuff since she had to take the bus home.

"Eeeww, you're getting it all over your hands!" Sue whined.

"So?" I didn't care.

"So, it's gross!"

"The picture or my fingers?"

"Eew! Both!"

I jokingly attacked her with my hands. Sue giggled, swatting me away. "Back, you beast!"

I retreated and wiped my hands on my jeans. Miss Finch, our English teacher, walked into the room. Everybody quieted down a little but still talked, since the bell hadn't rung yet. Miss Finch fussed with some papers on her desk and lightly touched her white halo of hair. She glanced up at us nervously, as if we were a pack of dogs that might snap at her if she wasn't watching.

"Guess who likes you." Sue turned back, whispering into my ear.

"Who?" I scooted closer, pretending to be interested. If she had said Randy or maybe Brad Hawkins, I would have melted through my seat. Of course she didn't say any guys' names. It was probably some cow like Lorna Seward, who took Home Ec and went to Donny Osmond concerts.

"Well, you have to guess!" she teased, as if I should be very much into this coy game.

"Whaddya want me to do, go through the whole yearbook?"

Girls were always calling me anonymously and asking me who I liked, ever since junior high. I guess I have one of those Bobby Sherman-type faces that girls go for. It was so dumb when they'd call. I could imagine them sitting on the bed in their mom's room at a slumber party, their friends giggling and painting their toenails and eating Cheetos. This girl business was a real drag, like when I was in a real awful play last year, memorizing lines I didn't want to say.

"Want me to give you a hint?" Sue asked.

I knew it wasn't her. She'd been dating Terry Simms all year. Terry was a wrestler and very sexy. He had a muscular butt and an uncircumcised penis which I'd memorized from glances in the gym class showers. He was also a really nice guy, which made him even more of a hunk.

The bell rang. Sue whispered a last tidbit before turning around. "She's got brown hair."

"You mean it's not Miss Finch? Oh, I'm heartbroken!"

I pretended to cry into my desk. Sue giggled some more. Everyone else saw me acting silly and stared, like, what a joker. I didn't care. I was getting an A in English. This was one of the few places where the jocks and the hoods and the popular crowd couldn't put me down.

Miss Finch "a-hem"ed everybody to attention. She overlooked my fooling around since my hand was always raised to answer questions. But she also picked the kids who didn't know a thing, trying to catch them. As if that would do any good. She started in on our assignment, *The Scarlet Letter*.

"I trust you've all read up to Chapter Six?"

Silence.

"Well, perhaps someone would like to summarize the events thus far."

I raised my hand. So did Sue and a few others. Miss Finch looked over the few raised hands. Satisfied with her meager garden, she still had to attend to a few weeds.

"Sam?"

Sam Wier looked up from the book he pretended to have been reading.

"Uh, well..." He looked around as if the answer was written on a wall somewhere. Randy and I had gone to a few rock concerts in Cleveland with Sam. He was a burnout, but not stupid.

"It's like, this lady with the tattoo, er the letter, she's goin' into town to get back at the preacher guy, an' she's walkin' with her kid, who's a bastard—"

Everybody laughed.

"Illegitimate," Miss Finch corrected him.

"Yeah, right." Sam was enjoying this. "Well, she don't care what other people think of her and the kid, even though the preacher guy is a real hypocrite an' wimps out—"

"What does that mean?" Miss Finch scrunched up her face.

"Well, you know, he couldn't deal with her gettin' pregnant, so he fakes off like it's not his problem. He dun' wanna deal with it 'cause since he's the preacher...well, he's the preacher."

"Well, yes, I guess that's something like it. And how does this relate to modern life?" Miss Finch looked around. Silence. I raised my hand.

"Yes, Tom?"

"Well, there's lots of people who maybe, uh, love somebody that society, they can't, like, they're not allowed to be together—"

Somebody made a whiny noise behind me, a cheap queer whiny noise, like I was talking about something dirty. I shut up.

"Do these attitudes prevail even in modern life?" Miss Finch asked me.

I could feel her looking at me, the whole class looking at me, like, go ahead, make a total ass of yourself, we can't wait.

"Sure..." I mumbled, digging my fingernail along the edge of my desk, cheap Formica-covered metal things you couldn't scratch your name on. I wanted to convert to shrink mode like in *Fantastic Voyage*. That would have been great right then.

Miss Finch went on asking questions. I wanted to spit in the face of whoever made that noise, and I hated myself for letting it get to me. I knew what it meant. The whole class knew what it meant.

I kept digging my fingernail into the edge of the desk. I sat like that, shutting out the whole room, until Miss Finch walked down my aisle, past me. I smelled light lavender. She walked back to Danny Umbrich, who had his head in his arms, hunched over asleep on his desk.

"Daniel?"

She leaned over him. He'd probably been out late partying the night before. When she didn't get an answer, she tapped him on the head, two little knocks. Everyone in class watched as he poked his head up, sleepy. His mouth hung open, and a big string of drool came out of his mouth. The whole class broke up laughing. Danny looked like a big baby, wiping his hand on his sleeve.

"You'll have to find a way to stay awake, young man," Miss Finch said as she trotted back up the aisle. She was a funny old gal, and continued with class like nothing happened. Kids made fun of her. She was small and frail. But nobody ever gave her any hassles. She'd probably have shattered like a China doll.

Some kids said she had a lover who died in World War II. That's why she never got married. She looked a lot older than she actually was, I think, because she didn't dye her hair like most of the old ladies in Plainfield did. I liked her, though, and told her after class once that I dug Hawthorne and had been to the House of Seven Gables in Salem on a family trip a few years back. I told her it was hard to get through all the old stuff, but it was worth it. She liked that, I think, even though it came out wrong. I think it's sad how great stuff goes over like a dud with other kids. Once I figured out *The Scarlet Letter* was about sex and all that, I got into it.

When the bell rang everybody immediately raced out of the room. I sat for a second and watched them all. I pretended I was in ultra-slow motion in another time zone. Little science fiction ideas like that used to keep me from getting too depressed in school, like with the chandelier in the auditorium. I imagined a *Phantom of the Opera* guy creeping around the school late at night, peeking out of a hole above the chandelier whenever I walked by. I was thinking about this when Sue gave me a friendly shove with her elbow.

"Her first initial is M," she said mysteriously, like we were spies exchanging a secret code. We headed out of class and I smiled at her, my detective cohort.

I asked; "Is it...Mary Magdalene?"

"No, silly!" She looked shocked. Kids slammed lockers in the hall, talked, walked by.

"Margie?"

"No."

"Melissa Duncan?"

"No. You like Melissa Duncan?" She hugged her books.

"No. What are you, crazy?"

Melissa Duncan played on the girls' basketball team. A total dyke. At least I thought so. But I didn't tell Sue. "Is it...Mae West?"

Sue stared at me. "Who?"

"Never mind."

I saw my sister Tara at her locker and thought of going over to say hello.

"I'll find out later," I told Sue.

"Okay," she said sing-songy. "But there's a dance next week, you know."

She went off down the hall and met up with Terry Simms, who looked like a short lumberjack in a red checked shirt. He kissed her, gave me a friendly wave, and they walked off down the hall. I wondered what Terry tasted like.

"Hey, handsome!"

I turned. It was Tara. She usually got pretty silly with me in school. We fought a lot at home, the usual sibling stuff, but in school we got along, kept a friendly truce. It was kind of fake, but okay, because she was popular. I called her Miss Everything. She was in National Honor Society and cheerleading, in French Club, Student Council President.

We were both on the Speech team, which was a lot of fun. Tara had encouraged me to join, which was nice of her. We got to go to other schools and meet kids from all over Ohio, even though we had to dress up and competitions started early on Saturday mornings. Tara was in debate, since she was into politics, while I found my groove in Oral Interpretation, reciting a short story, while some other kids would perform excerpts from plays.

Most of the other schools were a lot nicer than Plainfield's, but you could tell from the kids that it was the same hell, just a different box. I was on Student Council too, which sort of made me popular, but not real popular, just in the top bunch. Pretty stupid, huh?

"Hey, Miss Everything, Dad was pretty pissed at your stud and his Camaro this morning."

"Oh, I know. Shut up. Are you going home right after school?" she asked, going through her locker. It was neat and tidy with little flower cutouts and pictures of James Taylor and a mirror on the inside door.

"I guess so. Why?" I leaned against the locker next to hers.

"You forgot, didn't you?" She frowned.

Some girl I didn't know came up to us.

"Excuse me," she said. It was her locker I was leaning against, so I moved. Tara smiled and said hi to the girl by name, even though I bet she didn't even know her. She was always being nice to other kids like that, like a politician.

"Forgot what?"

"Dad's birthday!" She checked herself in the mirror.

Damn! I was supposed to make a card for Dad, a big drawing for Tara, Angelo, Mom and I to sign.

"Did you make the card yet?" She shut her locker door.

"No. I'll do it in art class."

"You better. Mom's getting the presents wrapped and everything today."

"What did we get him?"

Mom always bought our presents to Dad. It wasn't like it was a lie. She just knew what to get for him.

"A shirt, two ties and a sweater, I think."

"I'll get some big colored paper from art class."

"And I got him a plaque for his office, a bronze of that article about him in the paper."

"That was last month. The construction firm thing? Or the promotion?"

"The promotion. It meant a lot to him."

She started heading the other way down the hall. I sort of wanted to walk with her, all the popular kids saying hi, her being a senior. But I had to go the other way upstairs to French.

"It would have meant a lot if Rex had bashed into his car, too." I called out.

She ignored my joke. "Don't forget!"

We separated through the crowd of kids.

"I won't!" I yelled back, as I headed up the stairs and across the auditorium balcony.

Like I said before, our school was built around an opera house, so the classrooms surrounded the auditorium in a squared-off U shape. At the ends of the U, kids crossed through the seats on the first floor and across the balcony on the second. Usually there was a teacher out there to make sure kids don't skip class or fall off the balcony. I liked that part of the school, especially when we did good plays. If I didn't have to be onstage for a while, I'd sit back and watch the whole thing going on.

After classes, the school belonged to all the creative kids who stayed late. But it was bright daytime as I crossed the balcony. Out on the stage/gym, guys were lining up for gym class, wearing our school colors of geeky green and black shorts and T-shirts. Just passing by the gym gave me a queasy feeling in my stomach.

I walked looking sideways at the gym and didn't notice Joe Briggs coming the other way. He came up and bumped me hard, nearly knocking me over the balcony from behind. My books flew out of my arm. Of course, he was too tough to say "Excuse me," or just walk up another aisle. He grunted, turned to look at my books all over the aisle.

"Faggot."

I heard it loud and clear, turning away, picking up my books. I looked up, but no teacher was around. I watched him strut on ahead.

Joe Briggs was built solid. He had mean eyes, silvery like a wolf, and a big strong nose. He was really hot-looking, like in some porn magazine, except he was a mean bastard. I've seen a few porno magazines. At one of Ed Drake's basement gatherings when his parents weren't home, he showed me and a few other guys a few *Hustler* magazines as a joke, but it was gals with guys. I never got one; well, except a *Playgirl* I shoplifted. More on that later.

To be fair, Briggs did have reason to hate me.

The week before, Mr. Geissler moved gym class to the spare playing field next to the football stadium, which we apparently couldn't use, because the school spent so much money on the precious greens, and Plainfield College games were also played there. So we spent Monday, Wednesday and Friday playing flag football on the uneven grassy field.

The first day, little plastic strips tucked to the sides of my shorts like everyone else, I hung back, since football of any kind was foreign to me, and Mr. Geissler was a lousy teacher. He just had us split into sides and play.

As I trotted around, I kept hearing words like "flank" and "downs," and thankfully no one tossed the ball my way.

But by Wednesday, something clicked in my pervy mind as I watched other guys grab the plastic strips.

The point was to chase other guys' butts.

Being smaller, I raced unseen by others, and snagged my first "down," I guess.

Then, Terry Simms, on defense, got the ball and started running.

I hightailed it, huffing while zoning in on Terry's cute butt, until I finally yanked his "flag" off. He slowed his pace, turned and tossed the ball at me, grinning.

"Where ya been all this time, Tom?"

I shrugged, and grinned as he walked back after patting my butt.

Terry Simms patted my butt!

Friday couldn't have come soon enough. I was ready, and in a huddle, Dan Schotten said he might pull a surprise pass to little old me.

Some of the guys had figured out a way to cheat by tying their flag strips to their shorts, including Joe Briggs, who had yet to notice me at all. But when he got the ball, I raced to catch up to his muscled butt, but the fabric strips wouldn't pull off. I grabbed again, and Briggs tripped and fell, with me clutching that strip. His shorts tugged down to his jock strap, I fell on top of him, my face momentarily planted on his ass.

"Get the fuck off me!" Briggs shouted as he squirmed away, pulling his shorts up.

Stunned, I sat on the ground as laughter from almost everyone echoed across the field.

So that's why Joe Briggs hated me.

My moment of glory now days old, I sat in a balcony seat, just to take a breather after Joe's near-fatal revenge shove. My body was a mess, sweaty, hair all out of place, zits all over my back. I felt in my pocket. Forgot a comb again.

I sat and imagined jumping off the balcony. I'd have to land right on the aisle, not over a bunch of chairs. That way I'd look better when they found me, sprawled out, just a broken leg, maybe an arm, too. My right one. That way I could still write and eat and jerk off. And I'd tell everyone Joe Briggs pushed me over. Then he'd come into my hospital room to beat me up. But upon seeing me in my pathetic condition he'd feel ever so sorry, and he'd apologize and kiss me softly, his leather jacket brushing against my hospital gown.

Yeah, right.

The bell rang. I was gonna be late for French.

How could guys like that tell, I wondered as I rushed down the hall. Everybody called each other faggot, at least people they hated, but Joe Briggs said it like he knew, like he was naming a zoo exhibit, identifying the genus.

Where was the label that said, Look fellas! Right here! Spot the queer!?

It wasn't as if I faceplanted onto his butt on purpose, was it?

I wish I could have turned on infrared vision to see little green halos over every guy that was gay. With some guys it was easy to tell. Darin, of course. John Paley was one. He was a real queer, always lisping, in the Latin Club. I didn't like him and didn't feel obligated to like him either. I always tried to walk right and not swish around like he did. He even carried his books up against his chest like a girl.

Dad said not to let guys like Joe Briggs get to me.

"They're just assholes," he'd said.

"You try going to this school," I'd told him. "You try going where kids can find any reason to make fun of you, anything! A pimple! Your hair's messed up! Your shirt sleeves are rolled up wrong!"

Dad thought I exaggerated.

Randy Hartnell agreed with me. He was sort of my best friend, but he was a junior, so we only had choir together.

"Kids are awful here," he agreed. But he didn't care what anybody said. Like when he quit football in his sophomore year, just quit one day, walked off the practice field two days before Homecoming, and nobody hassled him about it.

Okay, Randy was more than a sort-of best friend. He was a friend I wanted to kiss.

Okay, more than kiss. I wanted to faceplant on his butt, on purpose.

3. Prokaryote

"Bonjour, mes amis!"

As the last student to get to French, my cheerful greeting was met with a variety of replies, all in French, none of them rude. It was mostly nerds and smart kids. We had big double-sized desks for two students each. Sometimes we'd break up in partners and do French conversations. Usually, we had quizzes and graded each other. Mrs. Purcell would look these over, but not take down our grades. I was feeling relieved when I sat down.

My partner was Karen Voss. She was a hood, sort of, with stringy black hair. Funny how you dump somebody into a group, but when you get to know them, the group label fades. Karen always chewed gum and got in trouble for it. She was also Joe Briggs's cousin.

That's one thing about Plainfield. You had to watch it when you were badmouthing somebody, because you were probably talking to his brother or sister. There was a lot of that. Niedermeyer, a tiny little town outside the county line off Route 42, had a population of sixty-four. Every resident was a Niedermeyer. They all looked alike too, skinny and long-faced.

"How ya doin' today, Tommy?" Karen asked, snapping her gum.

"Oh, terrific. Your wonderful cousin just nearly threw me off the balcony."

Mrs. Purcell sat at her desk, waiting for us to settle down so she could start class. The French room was filled with posters of France and cards with phrases that French people supposedly used a lot. Comme-ci, comme ca. C'en fais rien. C'est dommage.

"That Joey's a total brat. I hate that whole side of my family. I'll just have to go down the road tonight and give that boy a spanking." Karen grinned kind of nasty and popped a bubble.

I imagined Joe's muscular butt over my knee, waiting for the hard slap of my hand. I got a boner. I'd get a chance to see him naked in gym class today. If only I could just do the good part of gym class and not have to do basketball. At least nobody got tackled in basketball.

"Why does he hate me so much?"

She shrugged it off. "Oh, he's jus' jealous, y'know. You're so talented and popular."

"Me? Popular?"

"Sure, and he's ticked off about the gym class thing. Everyone heard about it."

"Oh, jeez."

"And you're different, too. You're not born here. He works on the farm and works on his car and that's it. He's always had to have somebody to pick on. Dun' even have a girlfriend."

"Vraisement?"

Mrs. Purcell took off her big cat glasses. "Preniez un papier."

That meant take out a piece of paper for a quiz. It would be a ten-question quiz. Mrs. Purcell made us tear sheets of paper in half and share them, like we were still living in World War II days and had to conserve stuff. I ripped out a piece and gave half to Karen.

"What does he do on the farm, wrestle cows?"

She smiled. "Something like that."

"The verb for 'to run,'" Mrs. Purcell announced.

Jeez, she was already into the quiz. I fumbled around with paper and a pencil. I looked over at Tom Conley, already writing. He wore Izods and L.L. Bean clothes before it became trendy. He'd already numbered his paper and finished conjugating the first verb. He was also one of the guys in school I figured was gay. We were sort of friends, but we never talked about it. There was just an unspoken understanding.

"The verb; to run." Mrs. Purcell repeated herself, overpronouncing the word. When kids asked her to repeat questions, they were obviously stalling. Either you knew it or you didn't. I knew this one. Courier. I imagined a cute French bellhop carrying a note and running.

"The verb for 'to sell.'" Mrs. Purcell peered out from behind her pile of books to see who was cheating. She talked a lot about her cats and plants and stuff that didn't relate much to French. She'd been there, though. She'd showed us pictures of her and Mr. Purcell, kind of fat and dumpy, standing in front of Montmartre and the Arc de Triomphe. Mr. Purcell looked tired, like he'd heard too many jokes about his name, "Mister Purse-shell." The French probably had a good time with their funny accents. They were from Cleveland, and said all the Rs hard and nasal.

"The verb for 'to sell.'" Easy. A guy who sells stuff at his little market is a vendor. Vendre.

Karen nudged me under the desk, her sign that I was supposed to let her peek at my test. I thought it was pretty pathetic she only got to question two before needing to cheat, but she nudged me again. I looked over at her paper. They were already on number nine! How could I space out like that? I quickly numbered my paper. I felt like a total ass asking Mrs. Purcell to repeat numbers three through nine.

She gave me a look, tired, as if I'd asked her to climb ten flights of stairs. She overpronounced everything like I was some kind of idiot. A few kids sighed, bored, waiting for me to catch up. I felt bad. All the Joe Briggs stuff nested in my gut like a knot.

Usually, French is easy. We stole a lot of words from them to make English. A lot of people don't know that. There's no such thing as a real American, except Indians. Everybody else is related to a bunch of thieves and criminals and leftovers that got kicked out of everyplace else.

We finished our quizzes. "Trade papers," Mrs. Purcell instructed. She seemed so tired of teaching, like she'd given up on something else a long time ago, maybe the hope of living in France. We traded papers, which meant this quiz didn't count. I was relieved and disappointed.

"Bear in mind," Mrs. Purcell warned. "Although I won't be scoring these, they're a good test of your vocabulary."

Right. I thought quizzes were dumb. We should have been learning how to talk so when we go to France, we'll be able to get around. I planned to go to Paris someday. Randy was into that, since he knew Jim Morrison died there. He wanted to go to his grave with me and do acid. I wanted to go with him, but also to meet some guy with sexy lips who'd take me to cafés where Picasso drew on the tables. There'd be sailors in striped shirts all horny over each other, but I'd go down a cobblestone street along the Seine. We'd stay in his creaky walk-up flat and make out and not even go to Montmartre or those silly tourist places, except maybe the Louvre.

We passed our papers up the aisles. Mrs. Purcell looked them over while we read aloud from our books. She half-listened. It made me sad to think how she'd been teaching so many years and didn't have to think much to do it.

We went from person to person, everybody doing a few paragraphs. The story was silly, about le Cote d'Azur, and how not to get sunburned. I was lucky. Somebody had scribbled the English translations between the lines. I read ahead to check out the new words. I was looking up maillot when Karen nudged me again.

It was my turn to read and there I was, Space Cadet. Karen pointed to where we were. I read it well, though, thinking about my dream beau mec and his sexy French lips, like Randy's, and the times I'd gone to Akron with Tara and her boyfriend Rex. We'd watched French movies to get the accents just right. I had wanted to ask Mrs. Purcell if she went to those movies. Some of them were kind of racy. She seemed prissy, though, and wouldn't teach us swear words. I bet she never saw an R-rated movie, French or English.

We finished reading. Mrs. Purcell talked about Quebec, how it's different from France, a kind of mini version of "the Old Country." Then she mentioned the quiz and how some people could have done better.

"Bear in mind, though, this is just a sample of what's to come," meaning there'd be a big test in a few days. She tried to scare us into studying harder. It usually worked.

Karen wrote me a note:

DONT WORRY ILL TELL JOE TO LEAVE YOU ALONE!
I wrote on the corner of my notebook:
NO!! DON'T SAY ANYTHING!!
She didn't know how that would make things worse, a girl defending me.
ITS OK I KNOW HOW TO DEAL WITH HIM
I wrote:
WELL I SURE DONT!

The bell again. The rumble of kids again. I heard the noise in the classroom mix in with the sound through the whole school, like once when I turned on the little alarm clock radio in my room and at the same time blasted the living room stereo, both playing the same station. There was a certain point on the stairs, where if you heard the two sounds, it made a lopsided earthquakey feeling.

"You coming?" Karen asked.

"Naw. Think I'll stick around and brownnose it a bit." I smiled at her, kind of fake, like Tara did.

"You're too much," she said with a smile and left. I scooped up my books and walked up to Mrs. Purcell.

"You know, Tom, you're a real disappointment today," she said without looking up. I glanced at the cards on the wall. Comme ci, comme ca. C'est dommage.

"I know, Madame Purcell." We called her that in class. When we joked about her, it was My-damn Purse-hell.

She looked up. "You should get your sister to help you. She's always doing excellent work."

Some teachers figure just because you're in the same family you all ought to be carbon copies. Boy, was Angelo in for a rough time here.

"I'll work harder, Madame, honest." Mrs. Purcell sighed. I started for the door.

"See that you do. Bonjour."

"Bonjour." Boneé jour. Boner jour. Boner journey.

4. Metaphase

I couldn't remember if it was Thursday or Friday. Was I supposed to go to Social Studies or Health? Then I remembered Darin telling me about gym class and got that bad feeling in my stomach. Friday. I wanted to see Randy, be near him, sitting by him in choir, our legs brushing against each other as we shared music scores.

Realizing I was going in the wrong direction, I stopped in the middle of the hall and bumped into Tracey Becker, one of the God Squad. I didn't say hi, just "Excuse me."

Health was Wednesday and Friday. I doublechecked the little schedule I had taped inside my notebook along with my locker combination. I had disguised the numbers like Elvish writing so no one else could read it. Of course, no one ever broke into my locker. The God Squad, however, often slipped little Christian comics in the locker slats so they'd fall out when you opened the door.

The God Squad was a clique of Grace Brethren kids who all got Born Again. They were each a bit snotty and holier-than-thou. It was creepy having them drop comics through the slats in my locker, like

I was on their Must Save list.

The comics were pretty ridiculous, talking about the Lake of Fire and how a peace sign is actually a broken upside-down cross and the symbol of the Antichrist. Dopey cartoon guys slap their wives and drink but find Jesus as their personal savior on the last page. I mean, do people believe this stuff?

On the back of every comic was an order form for more copies. I wanted to get a million so I could throw them in the trash, but that would be just as bad as what they did, burning books and records like idiots.

I liked to save these comics for Randy. He thought they were a real hoot. He was Christian, but not like the God Squad. It just came natural for him, liking God, but still partying. I appreciated that, since you could never tell who'd turn into a Born Again. One day a kid would be part of your crowd and then wham! They start acting snotty and try to get you to go to their meetings.

I went to a Christian students' prayer group meeting once with Greg Breyer in fifth grade. He's cute, blond hair, a tennis player. I had a crush on him. I went just to be with him. But all they did at the meeting was talk about how to get more members. They really missed the point. I read the Bible sometimes. Tara went to Presby and had a red-letter edition with everything Jesus said in red. I just read the red stuff. The rest is all second hand, isn't it?

The reason I'm going on about this stuff is that Mr. Wilbur, our Health teacher, was nutty on this stuff. Separation of church and state was a lost cause in Plainfield. They might as well have installed pews in the classrooms.

One year, the day before Christmas break, Mr. Wilbur gave out little crucifixes to his students, saying if you said or wrote "Xmas" instead of "Christmas," you were a Communist. Wilbur used to be the football coach, but he got fired after three losing seasons. We're talking 0-9, even though they prayed before each game. If God was on their side, then what was the other team, a bunch of Devil worshippers?

I went to Health without bothering to bring my book, since Wilbur would just read stuff out of it and blab at us. He managed to completely ignore the chapter about sex, which was actually what everybody needed to know about, at least birth control and diseases. More girls dropped out of school because of getting pregnant than for any other reason. *Please excuse Sissy from finishing high school. She is nursing and that takes up a lot of time.*

This Friday was the real topper. Dan Brock lumbered down in front of me. He was a big horse of a linebacker on the football team who ate two lunches a day, and was real good buddies with Brad Hawkins, probably.

Despite his three-year losing streak, the jocks in Health class thought Wilbur was totally cool, so anything a jock said in class was a real hit. Brock turned around and said, "Mollicelli, you're apathetic."

I knew he meant pathetic, but I wasn't about to correct him.

"So what?" I muttered, pretending to write something important in my notebook.

That didn't give him anything to start up with, so he just turned around. I looked at the hulk of his back. Green Dolphins jersey, 79. Terrific fashion statement. I swear, some guys just look for little guys to pick on for no reason. You could make them all disappear from the planet, and I don't think anybody'd mind.

Wilbur started up the class about acne. The book had a whole chapter on skin with terrific plastic layered pictures of hair follicles and sweat glands. It showed how if you popped zits too soon, they ruptured underneath you like little volcanoes. I had acne, but Dad took me to Cleveland every few months to see a dermatologist, who gave me lotion and soap and tetracycline. My face wasn't so bad. I never took the pills at school, though. Freddy Skaggs saw me taking some at the drinking fountain and called me a junkie. Freddy Skaggs got hit by a car.

No, he didn't.

But I wish he had.

"If you don't wash your face twice a day, you'll get what they call cysts," Wilbur announced. "I remember once my son popped a cyst, and the pus shot clear across the room!"

Can you believe a teacher saying this? Everybody grossed out.

The girls went, "Eeww!"

Dan Brock grunted a caveman laugh.

"Ew, grombice!" Karlene Hummel said.

Grombice was a word Karlene and her old crowd made up, or found in a book, I don't know which. It means gross, only worse. I thought it was dumb, her saying it, since it was a favorite word that unreligious kids used. Karlene used to be in the real popular crowd that set all the trends for the school, like stupid new words, or girls wearing little pom-poms on their shoes, or making their boyfriends wear suspenders. She and I used to be good friends. We'd hang out with Randy and his girlfriend, Shawna Braddon. We all did plays in junior high.

Shawna once told me Karlene liked me. We dated once, and I even kissed her at a cast party when we played Spin the Bottle. I liked it better when the bottle landed pointing at Randy. He and I kidded around a lot about being gay, except he didn't know I wasn't kidding. When the bottle landed pointing at him, we got silly and he reached over and planted a big smooch on my lips. It was great brushing against his stubble, everybody laughing and clapping. He tasted a lot better than Karlene.

Everybody got a big laugh out of it. I got a big hardon.

Karlene quit doing plays when she found Christ as her personal savior. It was too bad. She was a great witch in *Snow White*, the children's show we did for elementary schools. She had a crooked nose and long stringy hair. I guess she thought it wasn't popular enough to be in plays, so she got in the God Squad, then got in Student Council, then got elected Sophomore Class Vice-President. It was as if the God Squad thing wasn't at all what she felt. It was just a move on a chessboard.

"And if you pop pimples right here..." Wilbur made a little triangle between his eyebrows above his nose. "...you can get mental illness."

A couple of kids gasped.

"That's ridiculous." Sam Wier again. Quite an outspoken guy. Most teachers hated that.

"Okay, wise guy, prove me wrong." Wilbur puffed up his chest, sat on his desk, crossed his arms, and put his feet on top of the rims of his garbage can.

"It's just ridiculous," Sam said.

"Do you pop pimples up there?" Wilbur asked.

Sam frowned, already tired of the whole argument. "Sure."

"Well, there you go." Wilbur grinned, his dopey rubber face beaming.

Everybody laughed, except me and Sam, who made a move to get up, I don't know, to leave class or deck Wilbur. Either would have been okay by me. Instead, he hesitated and sank back down in his seat.

"I'm jus' kiddin' ya," Wilbur reassured him, like a guy who shoots you and then gives you a Band-Aid. "Enough of this pimple stuff. How about we talk about something else? How about continuing our discussion about this EVILooshun stuff? Anybody got inny ideas they wanna share?"

The guy was raring for an argument. He rubbed his hands together and bobbed his head up and down.

Nobody said anything, until Karlene Hummel raised her hand and said, "All I know is, my relatives aren't monkeys."

No, dear, they're baboons. Karlene smiled sassy like someone was supposed to give her a lollipop for answering correctly. It was like the time in advanced composition when Mrs. Coland asked somebody to make a simple subject-verb sentence. "Jesus wept," Karlene said, putting on the same lollipop face.

"Mollicelli, you're awful quiet. Not at all like your sister was."

"Nope, not at all."

31

"Wal, ain'chew on thu Debate Team er sumthin'?"
"Speech Team."
"Don'cha wanna debate this?"
"Not particularly."

I wasn't a debater. I performed a short story, but I was not about to correct him that I did Oral Interpretation.

"Huh. Ain't that sumthin'?"' Wilbur went on arguing with some other kids, talking, pretending to listen.

I saw a cartoon when I was very small. An ant's at a picnic. All the other ants are with him, towing away watermelons and plopping them down the anthole to the tune of jazzy 1940s music. A bunch of them carry off a big sweet drippy cake with a lot of white icing. The ants trip on a root and the cake flies back in the air, landing on the little ant, and plop! He's gone in a mountain of white icing.

Gone. Ha. Ha. That's all, folks.

5. Angiosperm

The art room was a sprawling chaos of unfinished paintings, ceramics wheels, and drawing boards; a sanctuary for lost causes. The smells of turpentine and clay mixed in a sharp incense that soothed and helped me forget the rest of the school.

Mrs. Taube was the best teacher in the school, short and pudgy with a high Minnie Mouse voice that could never be mean. She showed us how to do everything: Japanese watercolors, gauche, silk-screening, even painting with coffee grounds, a medium I was using to finish an old-fashioned Cezanne-type still life with apples and oranges.

I spent the first part of the period cutting a matte for painting. Mrs. Taube wrote up a little name tag and put it in the showcase in the hall outside the classroom. I was out in the hall showing it to Darin when Joe Briggs and some other hood, I forget his name, came up behind us.

"Ain't that cute," Briggs said. "The little faggot painted a picture."

The other guy dangled his keys, which hung from his belt loop.

If that guy had as many doors as he had keys, you'd think he'd be someplace else.

"Go to hell," I said to Briggs.

I started to head back in the art room. Briggs shoved me and I almost fell to the floor. Darin stood in the hall, not knowing what to do.

"Ya wanna start somethin'?" Briggs yelled, almost coming into the room.

Mrs. Taube got up from eating a sandwich at her desk.

"Do you have some business here, little boy?" she asked, looking up. Briggs was a whole foot taller than her, but he seemed small next to her. He cocked his head sideways.

"No." He stared at me over Mrs. Taube's head.

"Then why don't you just be on your way?" She stood at the door, guarding the fort.

Briggs walked away with his goon friend.

"Who's your buddy?" Darin sat down beside me at my table.

"Real funny."

"Real Funny. That's a real funny name."

I tried to appreciate Darin's attempt to cheer me up. I had hoped he might defend me, but Darin wasn't like that. Mrs. Taube went back to her sandwich as if nothing happened.

"Well, uh, I gotta get back to Social Studies. See ya after gym?" Darin looked out the door, wondering if Briggs might still be out there.

"Yeah, see ya. Uh, don' worry. I think he's picked his victim."

"He's an asshole."

"Yeah, right. Come and visit me in the hospital, okay?"

"Huh?"

"Forget it."

I tried to start up with an oil painting I was working on. Maybe I could finish it today and give it to Dad for his birthday, I thought. I wanted it to be really thick, like the paintings I'd seen in art books about the post-moderns. I kept messing up though, digging too deep with the palette knife, slopping the wrong colors around. Besides, I had to start on Dad's giant birthday card.

Tony Sheets came up to me. He was one of Randy's friends that I went to rock concerts with. He spent most of his art room time making ceramic bongs and ashtrays.

"You know something?" Tony said, crossing his arms over his Aerosmith T-shirt.

"What?"

"Briggs's allus bin a total sum'bitch. He gits on yer case agin, you jus' tell me." He gave me a pat on the back.

"Thanks." I swallowed hard, fighting back a sniffle.

"You jus' yell." Tony went back to the ceramics corner.

"Okay."

I imagined Tony stabbing Briggs and me dying in Tony's arms like Riff in West Side Story. I thought about dying like Bernardo, too, since I heard the guy who played him was gay. At least my mom told me.

She knew a lot about movies. We used to watch old movies together a lot in the summer. I think she knew about me. I had a *Playgirl* magazine under my mattress which she'd probably seen when she changed my sheets. My brother Angelo probably knew, too. He was very nosy, always getting into my things. It was tough trying to get some privacy to beat off since I shared a room.

He snuck up on me once. I was lying on the floor one afternoon with the magazine, and he came bounding in. I stood up with my pants around my ankles and kicked him out and slammed the door, screaming I'd hit him if he didn't leave. He was laughing and screaming and pushing on the door. Then he went downstairs making fake hard laughs. I slumped against the door. Over on the carpet lay the centerfold, a big lumberjack stud running around in the woods naked, his cock flopping around, free as a bird.

See, I stole the *Playgirl* from Bendico's candy store. He had a whole magazine rack full of porn magazines, but he never let kids near them. He stood guard every day. I could never see the covers clearly, the counter being in the way. I knew there were guy's magazines with naked women, but I didn't know there were gay magazines there too, so I never thought to get any of them.

But one day, on the rack right by the window, in between *Heavy Metal* and *National Lampoon*, was a *Playgirl* with a real sexy mustached guy on the cover. I guess Mr. Bendico didn't think it was a dirty magazine, because it was right out front, this stud staring me in the face every day when I walked home from school. Every day I went by, I knew inside the guy was naked.

One Saturday, I got the guts to steal it. I didn't go on a school day. Bendico watched for shoplifters like a hawk with all the other kids around. Only a few old guys sat at the counter, eating sandwiches. I stood around, pretending to read a *National Lampoon*, all the while peeking up at the mustached guy on the cover of the *Playgirl*. I carefully placed the *National Lampoon* on top of the *Playgirl*, then read another magazine and put it back.

Then I picked up the *National Lampoon* with the *Playgirl* underneath and walked down the book racks where Mr. Bendico couldn't see me. I slipped the *Playgirl* under my shirt and partway down my pants. I was nervous and sweaty. The cover of the magazine stuck to my back. I wondered if the guy's face would stick to my skin like a fake tattoo. The pounding in my chest seemed to blot out all sound from my ears. I went up to the counter and bought the *National Lampoon*, nearly forgetting my change.

I walked out feeling quite weird, as if at any moment I'd feel a bullet go through the magazine and into my back. It was awful to do, and I couldn't believe myself when I ducked into an alley on the way home and briefly flipped through the *Playgirl* before stuffing it into the bag with the *National Lampoon*. The thrill of that moment was as close to sex as I'd ever felt. I had a magazine with pictures of naked guys, their cocks out and everything.

Mom was in the basement doing laundry when I got home. Angelo was nowhere in sight. Dad was out on the lawn. Tara was out with Rex. Perfect. I went to my room and starting whacking off with the *Playgirl* and that's when Angelo barged in on me.

The bell for lunch rang. I decided to stay in the art room and skip lunch. Some other kids got out pack lunches and kept working on their stuff. I should have eaten something since my stomach growled like a sick cat, but I didn't want to go out to the auditorium and stare at the fart stains with Darin. The real reason was Briggs, out there, just beyond the fort wall.

After all the craziness with Briggs, I found out which girl liked me.

Sue Shumaker came by the art room door, giggling and screaming with Melanie Robbins. Sue shoved her in the door. "Tommy! Here she is!" Melanie ran back out of the room and they both rushed out of sight down the hall.

Mrs. Taube finished her lunch and rolled her lunch bag into a tube, filing it away to use again.

"Well," Mrs. Taube said. "You certainly are having a very unusual day."

"For sure." I looked at my painting, a corny beach scene. "You know, I think I might as well ditch this."

"Oh, no, you don't!" Mrs. Taube looked at me, astonished.

I smiled at her and started painting again, little strokes for the bird wings, dabs of white for the sea foam.

Mrs. Taube returned to my side. "Here, have an apple, at least."

"Thanks."

Melanie Robbins likes me. Pretty cute, for a girl. Cheerleader, JV though, not varsity. Melanie Robbins likes me. A lot of other guys would flip to get news like that. If I ask her to the dance next week, she'll say yes for sure. Melanie Robbins likes me.

Terrific. I'm so happy I could fall off my dinosaur.

6. Poikilothermic

In Algebra, there was a row of tall windows with beautiful trees outside. I spent most of fifth period staring at them, waiting for them to change colors and become snow covered like in *The Time Machine*. I used to think things like that a lot, real crazy, like, what would this school look like in a hundred years? What if they demolished the place and you could stand on the roof and watch the building crumble beneath you? What if you got a gigantic chainsaw and cut through the building like a pie? That'd be great!

Dad took me to a lot of construction sites. I know how a building looks on the inside, its skeleton. One guy on a site let me ride on his bulldozer. He was quite muscular and had a little hole in his jeans right in his crotch. I tried not to let him see me stealing looks at him, but he noticed and seemed to like it. He was really sweaty. The smell was overpowering, deep and smoky, not like the sweat of the boys' locker room, which was kind of sour.

The bell rang again. An entire hour had passed, and I hadn't even drawn a parallelogram. Oh, well, C- it shall be. On to Randy Hour.

The choir room was in the basement, past the wood shop and the wrestling room and a bunch of mysterious janitors' room. Mr. Howard's office overflowed with files of sheet music stacked up against the brown paneled walls. From his office, you could sneak up to the orchestra pit in the auditorium through a secret stairway, but kids weren't supposed to use it. There weren't any windows down there, which made the cruddy school smell stronger, like dust and sweat and raggedy newspapers.

A lot of guys and girls came to choir early, mostly because despite the dank room, it was fun. Most of them were nerdy guys I didn't know very well, like Rick Boyle, who threw up all over his desk in fifth grade. He did it right in front of me at Taft Elementary. I could never look at Rick Boyle without smirking, like barf might have come shooting out of his mouth any minute. He was really quirky too, like he never got over it.

Everybody who was in choir liked it. Some guys got a kind of "Aw, shucks" attitude and pretended to hate it. I will never understand that. Why can't you just say you love something if you love it, and not be fake about it?

Like Mr. Howard: he said we were the best choir around, and we were, practically. Our school had won a few of the state competitions a few years back. But he had a few kids in choir who couldn't sing, like Eddy Dunne, who was fat and sang like an old lady. I'm serious. I got in a fight with Eddy once in fourth grade on a field trip.

We went to a cookie factory, and he stole a cookie off the assembly line. I told him he'd mess up the machine because it would lose count. He told me to piss off.

Later, when we were eating lunch in a little park beside the factory, I teased him how he ate so much and stole cookies. He walloped me right in the head. I fell down and he started coming after me, but I grabbed his leg and bit him in the calf.

Boy, was that dumb. It took forever to live that down, sort of like Rick Boyle barfing, I guess.

I went to choir early. All the seats faced the door. If you were late, they'd all stare at you. I sang baritone and sat next to Randy Hartnell. He was the reason I liked choir the most. We were partners. Two kids shared a copy of all the songs. It was a big deal over who got the best copies. Some were old and marked up.

Mr. Howard had us make little marks, "lightly, in pencil, please." It was real serious business to sing right. If we messed around too much, he'd get very solemn and preachy and point with his glasses. Everybody wanted to be good, but when he made it seem like he was doing us a favor for being the choir director, I just tuned out. It was his job! They could replace him, but of course they didn't. He was a hometown boy, old money and all.

Every Christmas, he hauled us over to J. C. Breyer's big mansion on Country Club Lane where Plainfield's few rich people lived. We caroled for his big annual party of snobby cocktail adults. I really resented that, since we didn't even get asked to do it. It was like being a court jester for the local duke. J. C. Breyer practically owned the whole town of Plainfield. Half the cemetery was full of Breyers. He gave the choir a lot of money, which I think was illegal, but nobody said anything.

Half the people who would be calling this stuff out were at these parties, smoking and drinking, all the ladies wearing dresses that looked like lampshades and curtains. The decor was atrocious. I know that sounds really gay, but it's true. Fake ornate mirrors and wallpaper that looked like the set for a movie. I hate it when people with money don't know how to spend it. And they were soooo wonderful about "donating."

When we finished caroling, J.C. Breyer stood at the door and gave us a couple of dollars' worth of Wendy's coupons. Like, I am so thrilled. A Cheese Double with lettuce and tomato for missing *Barney Miller* and *Soap*.

There was also weird tension I'd get in choir, probably why it was great but a little awful. I loved sitting next to Randy. Sometimes when we sat next to each other singing, our legs touched, thigh against thigh, and Randy would keep it there. I could feel how warm he was, right through our pants. I always got hard. I didn't know if he did, though. I could tell he had a pretty sizable cock. He always had a noticeable bulge. I had never seen Randy naked. He was a year ahead, so we never had gym class together. By the time I got in high school, I never invited guys over for the night. I figured it was too gay. I think that was a big mistake.

Randy was very good-looking; shaggy blond hair like a surfer, big round blue eyes, a long nose and sexy thick lips. He was well built, softened a bit since he quit football and wrestling. "Got tired of sticking my face in ugly guys' crotches."

He said that a lot, accenting the "ugly" like maybe he wouldn't mind if the guys were cute. I don't know. Maybe I was just imagining that. A lot of things Randy said confused me. He said he loved me, but like a brother. We were drunk and just driving around one night. I wanted to tell him I already had a brother, thanks, and would he mind loving me differently. I didn't say it, though. I've got a lot of imagined conversations with people. They're up on a shelf in the back of my head behind my left ear.

One of these conversations was with Mr. Howard, where I tell him off for never giving me a solo, even though I got big parts in the junior high school musicals. I knew how he'd answer it. Shawna Braddon was in plays, too, and he told her we should be happy with the musicals. The choir stuff gives other kids a chance.

"It's their moment," he told Shawna. She did a terrific impersonation of Mr. Howard, pointing with glasses. It was too funny.

We bitched a lot about choir. Shawna and I both wanted to go to college and do theatre. We couldn't wait to get out of high school, away from people like Howard, who played favorites with all the jocks, especially Brian Leonard. I could just see Mr. Howard giving Brian a blow job after choir. I bet they were both gay. I imagined ten years after high school I'd go into a gay bar and see Brian in drag. I heard Howard was gay, even though he had a wife and two kids.

There was an old rumor about Howard getting caught in the bushes with one of his football buddies in high school. He also got caught at a rest stop outside of town. It was so weird, him being a popular guy. Then his family got disgraced and all of a sudden, he was married and working for the church choir. Then he was respectable again and teaching at school and a town big shot who got anything he wanted out of the school board. Everybody was a hypocrite in Plainfield.

Mr. Howard was going over a solo with Candy Barnard. Everybody chatted quietly. I told Randy about Joe Briggs. He immediately offered to beat him up for me.

"He is such an asswipe."

I agreed.

"Hey, you still wanna go camping this weekend?"

Once in a while we'd spend the night out at a cabin on his cousin's farm. There were a lot of woods around Plainfield, that and cornfields.

"Is Ed coming?" I asked.

Ed always went with us. Sometimes I wish he wouldn't so Randy and I could be alone. But Ed always had good pot and we had a good time.

"Sure, he'll come." Randy made a gesture like he was toking a joint. I smiled.

"I don't think so," I said. "I got a speech tournament in New Philly tomorrow."

"You're gonna miss a great time. Jack Adler's having a party. We could go to the cabin after that."

Jack Adler was the son of the biggest car dealer in town. They were quite rich and had a terrific modern house on Country Club Lane. Jack's parents were divorced, and his dad was never home. Jack had two rooms to himself and even a Space Invaders game, not just hooked up to the TV, but the whole machine.

I really wanted to go with Randy, but I had to go to the speech tournament. Well, I didn't have to go, like with sports if you skip, you'll get kicked off the team. I felt obligated. Sometimes other kids wouldn't be prepared, or they'd have other plans, and wouldn't go. Tara would get on my case about it, and Mrs. Schafer, our advisor, would be mad.

She was my favorite teacher other than Mrs. Taube, and she directed the two plays I was in last year. She said if we kept up the good work, we'd probably make it to the state speech tournament in Columbus.

"Besides, it's too cold," I said.

"No, it's not. It's only October. Remember when we went last February? It was great!"

We had made a lot of coffee that time. Ed brought his bow and arrow. We wrapped the points with oily rags and lit them, shooting high into the trees, watching them burn like meteors falling into the snow. It was fun, even though I froze my ass off. Pissing in the snow, making patterns, but Randy had his back turned, so I never got to see his dick. I did dopey macho things like that so Randy and Ed would like me.

"Lemme tell you after school!"

"Awright, you don' have to get upset," Randy said. He started looking through the sheet music.

I couldn't tell Randy that the real reason I wanted to compete in another speech tournament wasn't to win yet another tiny trophy or a medal, but for a guy named Chuck.

For the past several Saturday mornings, I had prepared myself to be ready to go at dawn in a jacket and tie under my coat. Mrs. Schafer picked me up with a few other students piled into her station wagon, while Tara and a few other seniors drove in someone else's car.

Three weeks before, I had been ready to do my usual performance in a classroom with five or six other competitors, with a teacher serving as a judge sitting in the back. I had decided to perform a Damon Knight short story, "To Serve Man," which of course was also adapted as a *Twilight Zone* episode, so some people knew the trick ending about the aliens' secret plans, while other didn't.

I pretty much knew the other competition. Antigone Girl overdid every line but got good scores. Freddy, the Black kid from Canton, did his James Baldwin speech quite well. He'd become my toughest competition, usually.

One phrase from his speech stuck in my mind from each of his recitations about Baldwin's "delusion as a little boy, that you would get what you wanted, and become what you said you were going to be, painlessly."

When I'd complimented Freddy on his performance after a round one week, I sort of joked that my own selection about aliens was "silly" by comparison.

He assessed me with both dismissal and a compliment, almost in his speech voice, saying, "But surely you know that it's a metaphor for fascism."

I didn't.

A few other kids' Oral Interps were barely listenable after the second or third time. The tedium was that you only competed against the same dozen or so kids, so you had to listen to their performances every week. Being trapped in a suit in a cold classroom prevented zoning out.

But three weeks into the season, this cute guy just showed up late like he was in the wrong room. He was wearing a jacket and tie like the other kids, and his dirty-blond hair was shaggy yet combed. His eyes sparkled like he had a sense of humor about the whole thing. He scoped out the room, each of us sitting quietly apart from each other, and sat down right beside me.

"I'm Chuck. Chuck Shaw." He offered his hand.

"Tom. Tom Mollicelli," I grinned as I shook it.

"Nice to meet ya, Tom Tom."

His smile, and his slight eyebrow raise, implied that there would be more to happen between us than joking about our names.

As I recited my story, and revealed the last line (Spoiler: the aliens' manual is a cookbook), Chuck gasped and giggled, which we're not supposed to do. He almost made me laugh as I nodded my head and sat down.

Then he got up next and did a very rousing version of a short story by Tennessee Williams called "Two on a Party." Since there's a strict time limit for speeches, he probably edited it, but I understood it was kind of sexy with two guys and a gal drinking their way down the east coast in a convertible, and it implied some kind of bisexual action. I mean, Tennessee Williams wasn't exactly appropriate for a high school speech competition, but he performed it with such a casual sense of humor, all while hitting different focal points for each character. I sensed strong competition. I could say goodbye to my tiny trophy, maybe a third place if I was lucky.

After our round finished, instead of leaving with the others, he smiled again, saying, "On to the next round!" He then made a sort of faux-formal gesture to escort me out.

As we walked down the hall like a hokey tour guide, he started talking about all kinds of stuff, even making a joke about his home town, Coshocton, as being "Show Cock Town." He gave me another little eyebrow raise as if that was some kind of clue.

"You're very good."

"Thanks. Chuck." I liked the sound of his name when I said it, solid.

"Are you a theatrical type?"

"What?"

"Acting, my man."

"I've been in a few plays," I said, blushing.

"Last spring, I was Sky Masterson in our school's truly horrid production of *Guys and Dolls*. I dreaded kissing my leading lady."

I stared at him.

He gritted his teeth. "Braces!"

My laughter bounced across the hallway, making other kids stare.

Each school's theater or auditorium usually became the closing gathering place where teams awaited the results, gathering in clannish packs with few exceptions. Chuck had continued our conversation and seemed to deliberately seat us apart from others. Before sitting, he peeled off his jacket and loosened his tie. I thought I caught a whiff of his cologne or deodorant. He slunk down in a seat, patting the one next to me, then loosened his tie. "So it begins. Waiting for god-awful."

He smirked at me, expecting a laugh at his pun.

We had only begun resuming our flirtatious chat when a shiny-faced blonde girl with a perky attitude plonked down facing us in the seat in front of us.

"Howja do, Charlie boy?"

"Don't call me that. Tom, this is Jennifer, one of our school's enthusiastic local organizational volunteers." He practically snarled it.

Having seen her onstage helping with lining the tiny trophies and ribbons at a table onstage, I didn't have to worry about saying anything rude, since Jennifer rattled off a series of gossip items about their school, pausing her not-subtle reminder of her need for a date to some school dance, only stopping when a teacher took to a microphone onstage.

I understood; she was Chuck's Melanie, only more assertive.

When our category was announced, Chuck placed third, I won second, and Freddy won first place; he a trophy, Chuck and I ribbons. As the three of us remained onstage for a photo (his school's yearbook and/or newspaper), he muttered, "When you talk about this, and you will, be kind."

He seemed to always be quoting lines from old movies. Chuck would later wrap the ribbon around his neck and jokingly imitate hanging himself.

For the next two weeks I looked forward to hearing his Williams short story yet again, and definitely got that there was a gay angle; the same thing with him. He didn't lisp. He wasn't fey, but his interest in me got me interested in getting my tired ass up at dawn to get to the next speech tournament.

In Zanesville, I won First, Freddy won second, but Chuck didn't place; damn that Antigone girl. Although we did have a bit of auditorium time together, he seemed disappointed.

At the tournament the next week in Wooster, he didn't show up. I kept glancing to the classroom door as I waited my turn each round. At the awards, I tried to seem casual as I approached one of his teammates to ask why Chuck hadn't shown.

"Dunno," he said. "I think he called in sick. Mighta quit."

I didn't even understand how or if we could ever be alone together, if I could get his phone number, meet some other way, to do what he kept hinting about.

Would he show up to compete tomorrow in New Philadelphia? I was damn sure not going to miss that opportunity even if he didn't show up, especially since Randy was closer, by my side three times a week at choir practice, but pretty much clueless about my feelings for him.

I wanted to explain it all, or part of it, to Randy, but Tammy Vogel came up to us. The girls all sat in the back of the choir room behind the guys. I swear Howard did that just so he could look at all the guys' crotches. All the girls were talking with each other. Shawna sat over with the sopranos on the other side of the room and waved at us. But Tammy was a real flirt and liked talking to guys better.

"Hey, studs," Tammy said to us.

"Hey, baby," I said to her, jokingly sexy.

"Scoot over."

I gave Tammy half my chair. She sat between Randy and I.

"I hear you've got a girlfriend," Tammy said coyly.

I glanced over at Melanie, who sat with the altos talking with

Lorna Finney. She glanced at me and smiled. I looked away.

"What's this?" Randy asked, surprised.

"Aw, you're nuts."

"Sue told me," Tammy confessed.

"Who's the lucky lady?" Randy asked me.

I didn't say anything. I pretended it wasn't a big deal when it was really just boring, and impossible, biologically.

Tammy got smarmy. "I know. It's Mel-on-eee!" She sang it high, which made us laugh. A couple of kids turned around. "Are you gonna ask her to the dance next week?"

"I don't know," I said, pretending to be cool. "I'll have to check my agenda."

"Aw," Randy gave me a little punch. "What a boner."

Tammy pretended to be shocked. "Such language!"

It was silly to see her acting like a prude, since everybody knew she and Jack Adler were a hot couple and probably had sex. Some girls act like they're on strings, little puppets. Tara acted like that a lot, a real performer at school, then she'd fall apart bawling to mom at home about something one of her supposed friends said about her, like when one of her supposed best friends said she didn't win Homecoming Queen because she was "too smart."

Another puppet was me, being nudged into asking Melanie on a date.

"Come on, people, let's settle down and get some work done." Mr. Howard called out.

Tammy got up. "You coming to our party?"

"You bet." Randy said.

I nodded. "You want us to bring something?"

"Eddie Drake." She giggled and went back to her seat.

Ed always brought dope to parties. Jack Adler usually had some too, but Tammy must have wanted the party to go well. She really made Jack's parties a hit. All her friends came, too. It was a lot more fun when girls were at parties. They brought food, and guys weren't as uptight. I learned you should eat when you party. I got sick a few times from drinking, which is another thing I used to do just to be liked.

The Drama Club went to see a play in Cleveland last spring. There were about ten of us. Ed Drake, who didn't act but was a great stagehand, asked if I was going in the "straight" car or the "party" car.

I didn't really understand, except that the straight car had Marty Schirmer, a jaunty jokester, Kelly Ritch, a mousey type, among others, and they were a bit nerdy. Ed was driving the party car and Shawna was going with them. Shawna said, "You wanna go with us."

I didn't know Shawna very well then, but she was quite fun at rehearsals, so I went in the party car. I don't remember the play because we were drunk and stoned before we got there. It was hard not laughing in the theatre.

The play was quite serious, but when they changed the set, the guy who was moving it got stuck onstage behind a flat. The dopey actor was awful, wiggling the platform with this guy making faces at him, caught on the door, waving to a techie offstage. Ed, Shawna and I were dying. Everybody kept shushing us. I thought they all knew we were high. My eyes probably looked bugged out like X-ray specs.

On the way back, we drank some more. Ed had brought a cooler full of beers. I lost count of how many I'd had, which was a mistake. Next thing I knew I was queasy and sweaty. I knew I was going to be sick. I rolled down the window and barfed all the way down the highway. It felt like some greasy monster grew out of my gut and punched his way up through my throat.

Before we got home, Ed stopped at Shawna's house and cleaned off the side of his car. He wasn't mad, though. I wish I could go back and erase some of the dumb things that happened to me. And not just a light eraser rub; hose down the entire chalkboard.

7. Interstimulus

Well, we played basketball in gym, but I didn't get to play. I never thought I'd long for more flag football.

We were all lined up when Mr. Geissler came out of his office with the student teacher Darin told me about.

Boy, was he good-looking, tall with sandy blond hair, almost red. His jawline was solid like Robert Redford, and he was built. He wore a mesh T-shirt that showed his chest underneath. His short trunks exposed a little untanned thigh. Usually, I had to concentrate not to throw a rod in the showers, but I really had to work not to get hard just standing in line.

Geissler bellowed; "Gentlemen, and others, this is Mr. Stoddard. He'll be teaching class today. You will give him as much respect and attention as you would me."

I'll give him more than that, you jerk.

Geissler handed Mr. Stoddard the gradebook and went back to his office. The school was always pulling stuff like that to keep you on your guard. Assemblies, fire drills. They herded us around like cattle.

Mr. Stoddard got down the line to me. He didn't look like a Mister, just a few years older than us, since he was a student at Plainfield College. He looked at me calmly, not mean like Geissler. His eyes were soft and blue. He looked a little nervous. My stomach was making noises from skipping lunch.

"Molliselli?"

People always said it wrong. There weren't too many Italian families in Plainfield. I expected Mr. Stoddard to make the usual gym teacher joke about my name sounding like a cheese.

"MolliCHELLi," I corrected him. I liked him even though he said my name wrong. His pecs were solid. Some of his chest hairs poked through the mesh T-shirt. It was very easy to imagine him naked. There was a guy in the *Playgirl* I'd stolen who looked a lot like him. I looked down at his shorts and thought, yeah, his cock's right there.

He smiled when I corrected him. "MolliCHELLi. Right." He checked my name in the gradebook. No cheese joke. Hooray.

Everything else was the same except a few new exercises Mr. Stoddard showed us. They were better, too. He showed us sit-ups that were slower and worked our abdominals more evenly. We split up in partners to hold each others' legs down.

Terry Simms gripped my calves, coaching me on. "Come on, Tom. Ten more."

He smiled as I wheezed in agony. "Do it for Melanie." I collapsed to the gym floor.

"Okay, switch!" Mr. Stoddard yelled.

Terry lay down, knees up. I held his legs, trying to savor every moment of being near him. His shorts tugged to one side, revealing the bulge where his jock strap stuck out. I will remember that vision forever.

We went on to wind sprints when a couple of jocks started horsing around. Jocks acted like they owned the place. Mr. Stoddard didn't know how to control them. Everyone was laughing.

Geissler came out of his office and yelled out, "Okay, you jokers! Twenty laps!" The guys went down into the auditorium and started running. It wasn't punishment for some of them since they ran miles every day for football. So did the track team guys in Spring.

Geissler headed back to his office, and then, just to get all of us, yelled, "EVERYBODY!"

Mr. Stoddard looked at us, sheepish, like he didn't know why, but we better get to it.

When it was too cold to use the playground, we ran around the outside aisles of the auditorium. Guys were always tripping on chairs. The floor was hard cement and inclined. The downhill was okay, but once you ran by the orchestra pit, ugh, back up the incline. I had no energy. I shouldn't have skipped lunch. Mrs. Taube's apple was long gone.

When I got up to the wall divider by the theatre's back doors, it was freezing cold. One of the janitors was fixing a door, holding it wide open. Nobody thought to ask him to close it, since we were just kids. Usually, the guys who run a place never know what they're doing.

It wouldn't have been so bad except Joe Briggs was in my gym class. He lapped me and gave me a big shove. I nearly fell to the concrete, but recovered. Then Eddy Dunne ran into me and I fell flat on my face with him on top of me.

"Goddammit, Mollicelli!" Eddy got up.

My T-shirt smelled like him, sour sweaty, fat sweat. All the guys in class lapped me. I knew I couldn't stop or I'd be a total wimp like Eric Hoffer, who said he had a heart condition and copped out on a lot of stuff. I felt like I was going to collapse.

I got up to the wall divider where the janitor was working on the door. It was freezing, but I didn't care. I had to stop. I leaned against the wall and bent my head down with my hands on my knees. My legs felt wobbly. The sweat of my T-shirt began to freeze.

Briggs ran by again.

"Can't take it, faggot?"

Brian Leonard ran by. "Come on, Mollicelli, or he'll make us all do more!"

He was right. Geissler figured that kind of stuff would make us all do better. It just made us hate each other.

Gasping and queasy, I started up running again. I clomped down the declining side aisle and stole a glance up at the chandelier. The Phantom of the Opera couldn't help me now. My ears were ringing. Little dots flew around in front of my eyes.

Finally, Mr. Stoddard whistled us in. I counted the five steps up to the gym floor and slowly made my way back to the clump of guys assembling around Mr. Stoddard.

Basketball. We have to do basketball now. Rex's coaching didn't help. Can't I just go?

We picked sides. I got picked second to last, Brian Leonard looking like he'd just inherited a leper. My jock credit from last week had faded to nothing. I felt very strange, relieved that I wasn't moving, cold and sweating at the same time. Mr. Stoddard got us in a circle and started talking.

I didn't hear him. The ringing and the dots came back and my knees wobbled and I felt a real cool breeze.

8. Predation

The real cool breeze was air whooshing by on my face's way to the floor.

I woke up on a table in a little room next to the showers. Bandages and towels were stacked on shelves. An empty whirlpool sat in the corner. I lay on a leather padded doctor's table. I had never seen this room. Jeff Roepke looked over me and was about to put a towel on my forehead when I woke up.

"How ya feelin'?" he asked. Jeff was manager of the basketball team and a gym cadet. He handed out towels and stuff.

"Uh, okay, I guess." I sat up slowly.

"Boy, you dropped like a rock. You sick or something?"

"Yeah, sort of."

Jeff leaned against the examining table. "Boy, you shoulda seen Stoddard. Scared shitless. Thought you'd died or something.' 'Get Coach Geissler!' he goes. 'Where's Coach Geissler?' Freaked out, then he carried you down here."

Wow, he carried me in his arms. That would have been real

romantic. I had to pass out and miss that.

"You're sposed to stay down here 'til you feel better. You can go if you wanna." Jeff was being nice to me, probably just to get out of being upstairs. "You wanna go to the nurse?"

The thought of going upstairs made me nervous again. "Naw, I'm okay."

"Well, I gotta get back upstairs. You take it easy. Jus' set there awhile." He pointed to me like a stern doctor.

After he left, I got up and walked around the room, nosing around the shelves full of bandages, tape, knee braces. I had only been down here when it was noisy and full of guys all rushing to get dressed and upstairs. Their feet echoed above me, tromping across the gym floor. Occasionally Stoddard tweeted a whistle.

Wow, Stoddard carried me. Totally dreamy.

The showers dripped slowly. If I could have turned invisible and just watched what went on there all day, the soapy combinations of guys, I would have been in heaven. It was a bit creepy being alone in there, thinking how I was so afraid of it and hated it, yet every night I'd return there in my mind, all those guys, wet and naked, cocks bobbing around, asses bent over. I thought if I worked really hard, I could pretend to like a sport and make friends with some of these guys, maybe just one. Some of them had to be like me inside.

I remember at Taft elementary school there were doors on either side of the gym. The doors went down some stairs. I'd sit on the bleachers with most of the other kids, waiting for the principal to call our bus numbers. Once I almost missed my bus. I got caught up watching a bunch of sixth graders run down those steps, one taking off his shirt as he trotted down into the mysterious room. I had no idea it was a locker room and they were changing for little league baseball. I just knew part of me wanted to go down there, and the other part was absolutely terrified.

I slowly walked around the lockers. Some of the doors hung half open. Inside one hung a red checked flannel shirt, Terry Simms' shirt.

I crept over to his locker, easing the creaky door open. Reaching out for the soft sleeve, I carefully took it off the hook and pressed it to my face. Warm smells of sweat and Mennen Speed Stick clung to the inside of his sleeve. I took a strong inhale, savoring his aroma, and replaced his shirt on its hook. I looked down in the bottom of the locker. His white Jockey shorts lay over his gym bag. I thought about picking them up. My cock was throbbing. No, I thought. Stop.

I walked over to my locker and sat, thinking through ways to escape. I could ask Randy to bring his hunting rifle on our camping trip. An accident. Walk out in the road. Get hit by a truck.

No, too messy. What if Randy really felt something for me, or Terry Simms, or... How stupid, how totally dumb. The only gay guys in that school were the fags like Eric Hoffer and John Paley and Tom Wiesner.

And me.

I lost track of time. All the guys in class came rumbling down the stairs. My first thought was to hide in the training room. I wish I had. Instead, I just rushed to my locker and tried to get out of there as quickly as possible. Most guys just ignored me, but it sounded as if every laugh were aimed right at me.

Briggs came up and shoved me and said, "Whassa matter, pussy wop? Din' Mommy give you enough milk today?"

He faked a punch. I scrunched up. He laughed, like I wasn't even worth hitting. "I'll take care of you later."

I dressed slowly, not caring if I ever got out. That was it. I'd go home and eat a box of laundry detergent. That would do it.

Most of the guys had gone as I trod upstairs to leave. Walking by the office, I thought maybe I'd go in and have a nice chat with Mr. Stoddard and he'd inspire me to become a great athlete who goes on to win at the Olympics. The whole thing started sounding like a toothpaste commercial so I just walked out.

I could feel all the kids' eyes taking me in, giggling about what I did. I walked down the paths the gossipy mouths made.

Guess what Mollicelli did? Didja hear? The wimp passed out in gym class! What a fag!

I kept hearing my name rattle inside my head in the bitter sixteen-year-old way that kids can say your name so mean it burns and you hate to hear it.

I slumped into my seat in Social Studies. I stank, since I hadn't showered. My hair looked like a rat's nest. No comb again. I guess Mr. Clutter stared at me as I walked in. He stopped talking. I didn't look up.

I opened my book to a page with numbers. Kids asked questions. Mr. Clutter wrote words in chalk. Kids wrote words and dates. Mr. Clutter wrote numbers that gave birth to more numbers. I doodled hard brittle lines on my notebook, an evil ice palace growing up around the sides of my Frazetta guy. All hope was lost for him. The ice palace grew harder. My pencil lead broke.

I looked up at the clock. Was I going to run all the way home, wee, wee, wee? Or was I going to wait Briggs out? Maybe I could just hide in my locker until graduation.

The electric second hand scraped around the clock face on the wall. My idea of time seemed quite messed up. It seemed to me time went the other way, counter-clockwise, with a yearly calendar on a huge circle. Winter goes at the top like the North Pole. Spring is a fun slide that takes you all the way down to the lazy green bottom of summer. Then you have to climb up to autumn, pulling on dying leaves to make your way back uphill again. So, time goes the opposite way than a clock.

Of course, if you were on the other side of the clock, it would go the right way, if you lived in the wall. Why does a clock go clockwise? Who decided these things? Why is this year numbered after some guy who died in Israel when half the world is already up to the 5,000s?

The bell again. The roar again, only triumphantly louder to the last, seventh period. Biology and Mr. Rick's green corduroys couldn't save me.

Escape swiftly, I thought. Sift in and out among the crowd of kids.

I trotted to my locker only to be greeted by the menacing face of Joe Briggs. I wanted to say something silly like, "Dear, we can't keep meeting like this. People will say we're in love," but I don't think he would have appreciated the joke. Bullies are not known for their wit.

"Going home early, pussy?" He hovered over me, preventing me from getting to my locker.

"Go to Hell," I muttered.

"What's that?"

"Go to Hell," I said, attempting to sound mean, but 'Hell' came out high-pitched, as if I was reading a Monopoly card.

Go to HELL! Go directly to HELL! Do not collect two hundred dollars.

I turned away from Briggs, accepting the idea of simply skipping Biology and going home without a coat and just the books I had. I wouldn't be returning anyway. I had a date with a box of detergent.

My back felt wide open as I headed down the hall away from him. A big red bull's eye appeared on my back, waiting for Mr. Bendico's bullet to finally get revenge for stealing that *Playgirl*. Instead, Wham! A thud in my back like an A.C.M.E. catapult, leaving me, Wile E. Coyote, sprawled over the hall in a puddle of books and papers.

Kids have a pretty quick scent for violence. Before I had even stood up, about two dozen guys had surrounded me and Briggs into a human boxing ring. Walking away would have been ridiculous, more shameful than my face getting beat in. I hated all the other kids more than Briggs for forcing me into a fight. The hate turned into adrenaline. All those years of watching *The Wild, Wild West* in reruns shouldn't go for nothing, I reckoned.

Briggs yelled for me to get up. I lunged up from the floor and shoved my head into his stomach, which took him by surprise, knocking him down. I was on top of him, and went to swing and punch him right in the face, but my fist slammed on the brakes just before impact on his handsomely cruel face. My fist just said, "Uh, no," to the rest of my body and sort of nubbed Briggs' face.

That gave him enough time to twist around and grab me by the neck. He began pummeling my face and ears. He struck gold, or red, with a knock to my forehead as I felt something wet; my own blood dripping down over one eyebrow.

I was thinking about how to grab Briggs' legs and knock him down again, when I heard a shrill familiar female voice.

"YOU GET YOUR HANDS OFF MY BROTHER, YOU GODDAM SONOFABITCH!!!!"

At first, I was quite embarrassed to see my sister Tara standing above me, her face beet red. But then I felt Briggs' grip release and turned to see Tara's boyfriend Rex clutching him by the neck and Briggs dangling like a puppy.

When I saw Rex slam Briggs against a locker and let him slump to the floor, I realized that when the President of the Student Council calls some guy a goddamn son of a bitch, she's probably right.

9. Geotropism

Mr. Bower was not a chummy Vice-Principal. Mr. Bower was a bulldog in a suit. Every kid was trouble to him. I should have known he wouldn't go for my sob story (I was very near tears) about not starting the fight.

After getting cleaned up in the nurse's office with some disinfectant and a bandage, I was escorted to Bower's office where Briggs sat in one chair. After I sat on the other, I scooted mine further from Briggs, who offered a smug grin.

Bower rambled on for a while about "discipline" and "behavior" in the voice of a cigar if it talked. I waited for him to ask us for an explanation.

Briggs shrugged.

"Look at me." I pleaded with him, pointing to my fresh bandage. "Am I the kind of guy who goes around starting fights?"

Briggs grunted, quite relaxed and content now that the whole thing was over.

Hey, baby, it's done. Want a cigarette?

61

He made no excuses. "Sure, I hit him. Am I gonna get suspended?"

Yes, and you're getting ice cream just as soon as you finish your vegetables, Bower seemed to think.

I took another angle. "Mr. Bower, if you were a cop, would you arrest the guy who got robbed?"

Not one for analogy, Bower gave us both three-day suspensions.

Damn. The worst part was, I would miss Mr. Hirsch' Biology class, and it was green corduroy day.

It was kind of odd being let out of school early to go home with this information. Ours was a household where A papers and watercolors were passed around the dinner table and posted on the refrigerator with little fruit-shaped magnets.

So, when Tara and I gave Mom, Dad and Angelo the play-by-play over supper, they were bewildered and amused.

"Three days?" Dad was confused. "What about your homework?"

"I'll catch up." I'd been farther behind without being absent.

"How could that vice-principal do that to you? Didn't you explain, talk to him? Reason with him? Why didn't they call us?" Mom cleared the dishes.

"Mom, you don't explain things to Mr. Bower. He doesn't deal with humans very often. They feed him raw meat for lunch."

Everybody laughed.

"He's not that bad," Tara said.

"Miss Everything, the Brownie points girl." I scowled.

"That's enough," Mom warned. "Give me your dishes."

We got up from the table.

Mom said, "You know, hon, you ought to take your son out back and show him how to defend himself."

"Sure," Dad offered. "How about it? I got into a few fights myself in the streets of Brooklyn." We sat in the living room.

"I think it's a little too late for that," I said.

"Well, whatever."

Dad unfolded his newspaper, a little relieved not to have to play boxing instructor. His presents lay on the coffee table next to him along with the card I made and the still drying beach painting Tara had to retrieve from the art room, due to my abrupt departure. He said he liked it. Mom would probably hang it upstairs in their room, on display but out of the way.

"It certainly is a pretty unusual birthday present."

Dad seemed a little bit proud that I had gotten in a fight, as if all the artistic stuff was okay, but getting in a fight showed that I was real, not some mutant who holed up in my room and made drawings. He was as proud of my black eye as I was, but neither of us could show it.

I got up and went upstairs to my bedroom. On the bottom row of my bookshelf, behind a Tolkein trilogy and a *Famous Monsters of Filmland*, I found what I was looking for: *Self Defense Made Easy*, a trim paperback book filled with black and white photos of guys doing throws, kicks and punches.

Chapter One began nobly.

"There comes a time in every young man's life when he needs to defend himself, his honor, perhaps even his own life or the lives of others..."

I flipped through the bottom pages. A frame-by-frame Karate move creeped along under my thumb like an old silent movie. I stood up and tried out a few of the poses. Kick the left leg. Punch with the right, defending with the left.

"Hey, it's Pete the Dog!" I turned to see Angelo peeking in the bedroom door.

"Get outta here!"

"My room, too!" He bounded over to his bed, reclaiming his half.

"Jus' keep quiet or you'll have two of these." I looked in the mirror over my dresser to examine my black eye.

"Tara said you got pounded."

"Shut up." My left eye was still puffy and dramatically blackened.

"I woulda creamed him," Angelo said. He leafed through a

Spider-Man comic book.

"No, you wouldn't've. You'd wimp out." I gave up admiring my wound in the mirror and slumped over to my bed.

"Like you." Angelo hid behind a Spider-Man comic book.

"Shut yer face, dipstick."

"Wimp."

I imagined hitting Angelo. That would be too easy, taking it all out on him. I thought of doing some homework, but remembered I didn't need to have anything done until Wednesday. It was over at least. Briggs wasn't going to bother me anymore. I could tell. He'd proven whatever sick point he had to make to himself.

I was supposed to be grounded for the duration of the suspension. I didn't feel like going anywhere, so it didn't matter. I went back downstairs and watched TV. I noticed the techniques in the fight scenes, compared styles, saw things I should have done. I tried not to get depressed about all the boys and girls together. I watch TV like an aquarium. It's life, but not a life I live.

Where are the happy gay people? Once in a while there's a prissy fairy on a game show or an old movie where a guy dies. But in the main time, it's all girls smooching guys and toothpaste commercials.

Some people think homosexuals hate women. Well, I don't. I just get tired of watching TV people fall in love and kiss and always having to pretend the girl's not there and the guy's kissing me. I like being a guy. Pretending you've got the girl's part is boring. That's what I hate, not the girls.

As a game show blared on the TV, I imagined Mr. Stoddard saving me from battle with the evil warlord Briggs. We tie Briggs to a tree and pee on him and get on our horses and ride out into Middle Earth for romance and adventure.

I futzed around the house, trying to forget about school until Randy called me.

"Hey, dude, how's yer day off been?" Randy's voice asked.

"Aw, pretty good. Did absolutely nothing."

"Great. You gonna party with us?"

"Wait a minute." I called out to the living room. "Can I go out tonight?"

"We're goin' camping, too," Randy reminded me.

"And then camping with Randy?"

I had Mom and Dad down with a simple system Tara used. Whenever we wanted something quickly, we'd make sure they were both in the same room. They'd give each other a glance like, I don't wanna be the bad guy, do you? Then we'd get what we wanted. Parent psychology is a very delicate art form.

"Don't you have a speech tournament in the morning?" Mom asked, confused.

Damn! I forgot to call Mrs. Schafer!

"Uh, I can't go since I'm suspended." I offered an impish grin.

"Well, I suppose our little mugging victim needs a little R and R," Dad said from behind his newspaper.

"Thanks!" I went back to the phone. "Good news, dude. We're a team."

"Great," Randy's voice said. "Pick you up later on."

"Later."

I got a little jump in my stomach, excited about the evening. Friday night, a starting bullet for the weekend. Even when I had nothing to do, I got totally hyped up on a Friday night. It was best to be in a car with friends, smoking and running around, but that didn't happen every Friday.

Most times in the early evening I'd be up in my room playing air guitar with Dad's T-square. Sometimes I'd catch Angelo at it, too.

After fussing around with my hair and popping a few little volcanoes, I brushed my teeth and sat down in the living room and wait for Randy. I got hungry and ate some cookies so I had to brush my teeth again. I'm weird about that. I hate going out with crud in my mouth, even if I'm going out for dinner. It's kind of gross, that first taste of food and toothpaste or beer and toothpaste, but it's like starting with a clean slate on my taste buds, even though the toothpaste tastes like candy.

I bet some really hotshot dentists got together one day and invented a toothpaste that makes your teeth fall out. That's how they make all their money. Angelo's orthodontist has a huge house, ugly too, with fake modern columns and ridiculous gothic arches. Angelo figured his mouth paid for the garage and one column. I'm not sure if that's true, but it was fun to think so when we toilet-papered his house last Halloween.

10. Polymorphism

A little after eight o'clock, Randy honked his horn in the driveway. I grabbed my sleeping bag and coat and dashed out.

"How's it goin', champ?"

"Huh? Oh, heck, lay off."

I slammed the door and lit one of Randy's cigarettes as we pulled out of the driveway. He pressed his cassette player on and Led Zeppelin's "Black Dog" filled Randy's car.

Play-acting again, I filled the role. I was never happier than to ride shotgun with Randy driving. His thick callused fingers held the wheel lightly. Control doesn't need to show its strength.

We got a little stoned and picked up a six-pack before going to Shawna's. When we got there, her mom sat with us and chatted like we were such nice boys. The furniture in the living room was like fake French Provincial. The room was quite clean though, the kind of clean where you know they never use the room, except for formal chit-chat scenes like these.

I smiled and nodded while Randy charmed Mrs. Braddon like I

bet he always did, since Shawna seemed to get her mom's approval regarding Randy. Looking at Mrs. Braddon and being quite stoned, I tried to see the little high school girl under all her fat and polyester and glue-dried hair. I tried to imagine her getting it on with Mr. Braddon in a '55 Chevy. I kept smiling until I realized Mrs. Braddon was talking seriously about something on the TV.

"It's awful," she said, shaking her head carefully. If she moved too fast it seemed her hairdo would fall off in a big clump.

"Why do they have to be so violent? Of course it's their own fault. Doing all those horrible things with each other."

I wasn't sure what she was talking about, but I didn't like her all of a sudden. I looked over at Randy. He was nodding his head, just listening but not agreeing, glancing distractedly at the TV. Some guys were getting arrested for protesting. Gay guys protesting in San Francisco.

I froze.

Mrs. Braddon continued. "Well, it's a good thing the police are arresting them. Might as well put them all—"

"Is Mom boring you with all her lectures?"

Shawna came down the stairs, looking great, as usual. Even though I know I liked guys, I loved seeing girls in those tight jeans, their butts shaped like cellos, curly and all. It was like I understood straight guys. As we got up to leave, I caught a whiff of her perfume.

"Ya'll have a good time, and be careful," Mrs. Braddon called out as we left. I was glad to be out of the house. The cold air felt good.

I sat in the back seat resting my arms on the front car seat. Randy lit up a joint. We cruised around and smoked, playing tapes and talking to other kids in their cars doing the same thing, all of us tooling around town.

Plainfield's main drag started in the downtown area which had a bunch of the usual stores with brick-faced buildings like an old Western, only instead of a saloon or a blacksmith there was a Thom McCann's or a JC Penny. Out of the downtown area ran Grey Avenue, a four-lane road that cut through the center of town all the way to Route 42 past the radio station which led you to Lincoln.

Plainfield used to be the real hopping town around the beginning of the century. Mr. Burns, my U.S. History teacher from last year, shared his local tales when the Revolutionary War seemed to bore him.

Kids from all the little towns like Birds Run and Kimbolton came to Plainfield for a good time. By my time, most kids with access to a car trekked to Coshocton or Zanesville. I'm not sure what it is they thought they'd find. You couldn't get any beer without an ID. When I didn't go out with Randy or someone older, I'd use a fake ID I sent away for in the back of a *National Lampoon*. It got me a sixpack at a few of the beer drive-thrus along Grey Avenue, in between the McDonald's and the Shoe World.

Lots of kids raced their cars up and down Grey Avenue. Mustangs were considered a cool car, also Camaros, Firebirds especially. They got tickets a lot, too. The cops didn't have much else to do but pull over kids' cars up and down Grey Avenue.

Randy handed me a second beer and we cruised for a while. Steve Miller Band's "Fly Like an Eagle" pumped out of his tape deck. It was starting to be a very good evening. Shawna started up about the stuff her mother was talking about, and in the middle of passing me the joint she said, "I hate fags," and I realized she didn't have the slightest idea about me.

How could she be interested in theater and be so clueless?

I toked on the joint. My head felt very big, like it might explode, or like in *I Married a Creature from Outer Space*, my pretty Thomas Tryon face would melt off and they'd freak out at my true identity. Come to think of it, that would have been a lot easier to deal with. Just hop on my spaceship and take off.

By the time we got to the party, I was pretty buzzed. When we came in everybody treated me like a big celebrity and how flipped it was that such a popular guy would get suspended. My bandage became a badge of honor.

The popular part sounded funny, but then I realized that most all the popular kids were at this party, and I was there, so I must not be such a bad guy.

"Some shiner you got there," Terry Simms complimented.

"Real souvenir," I joked.

"You oughtta lemme give you some boxing lessons some time," he said. "For next time."

"There isn't gonna be a next time," I told him, immediately regretting saying that. An invitation to box with Terry. I shouldn't have turned him down.

Everybody was drinking and shouting over the music. Tammy Vogel passed bowls of chips and pretzels, as if Jack Adler's dad never lived there, and Tammy and Jack were a happily married couple, him playing cards with a quartet of guys in the dining room. Some of the kids messed around with the stereo and the VCR and the video game in Jack's den. I saw Melanie Robbins standing with some girls and figured, what the hell, go along with it, she seems nice, get it over with.

"How ya doin', Melanie?" I shouted over the music.

"Wemishooinkyrededay."

"Huh?" I cupped my hand to my ear. She leaned in close. She smelled like Shawna, only lighter, sweeter.

"WE MISSED YOU IN BIOLOGY TODAY!" She pulled back, a little embarrassed about screaming into my ear.

"Oh, yeah," I smiled.

"Does your eye hurt?"

"Huh?"

"DOES YOUR–" she pointed to my face.

"Oh, no, not anymore."

I told her about Angelo calling me Pete the Dog from *The Little Rascals*, and some other cute stuff. She smiled nicely. I got her a beer, which she sipped like it was champagne. I was about to get really bored when someone put on Sweet's "Fox on the Run."

Shawna came up and grabbed me and we started dancing, the only kids on the floor at first, then everybody joined us, bouncing around and singing along, a few screeching out the high notes.

'I don't wanna know your name...'

Everybody hooted and yelled. Shawna and I swayed to the beat, flirting, bouncing around.

"Take a run and hide yourself away..."

I started spinning around and fell down, pulling Shawna with me. It was great to be so silly and crazy. I imagined everyone liking each other and everybody getting someone to be with. In the middle of all of it, I felt...I don't know, hopeful.

The song finished and everybody hooted and clapped. Shawna and I bowed dramatically and headed for the porch.

"Wait a minute," I called out. "I'm gonna get another beer."

I scooted around a dozen or so kids hanging out in the kitchen, sitting on the counter, eating food. It never fails. Throw a party, set up a hundred chairs, and the kids'll hang out in the kitchen all night long.

I pulled a beer from the case in the fridge. I joined Ed, who sat at the kitchen table rolling joints. He used a Yes album to scrape the seeds.

"Well, here's the Man of Eternity and fractions thereof." I set my beer on the table.

"To-mas !" Ed said my name like an Italian grandfather. He'd lived in Cleveland and was one of few kids who understood the whole deal of being Italian, even though he was German. "Are you partaking of the weed this evening?"

"Act Two. Need you ask?" I picked a freshly rolled pin joint, lit it, and inhaled. It tasted better than Randy's, juicier, more pungent. Ed's pot came from mysterious places, all below the American border, somewhere from the deep regions of Brazil, or so he claimed.

"Jus' get here?"

"No, we been messin' around out in the room of living."

The music kept up its insistence, but I could hear Ed clearly in the enclave of the kitchen.

"Nearly got bashed by the fuzz earlier." Ed rolled his tongue along the gummed paper of yet another joint.

"Really? what happened?"

"Aw, I got pulled over for speeding. Damn asshole didn't know I had all this lovely weed in my pocket." He pointed to the Ziplock bag full of human catnip. "I couldn't see a fuckin' thing through those Fascist sunglasses. I swear they don't have eyes, those robots."

"Stormtroopers."

"Taste Patrol."

"Sex Patrol."

"They're coming," Ed sipped a beer, leaning his lanky frame against the chair.

"When?" I asked, stoned to the state of total vulnerability, where joy and fear mixed in a cheap Op Art mess in my head and stomach.

"Any day now, Thomas." Ed's eyes took on a looming glow. "Did I tell you about the dream I had about you?"

"No." I leaned close to him.

"We were partying at somebody's house. It was like mine, but then you know how walls and floors move around in dreams. All of a sudden, we're in this big modern living room with glass walls on three sides, and glass window shades, like Venetian blinds."

"Yeah."

"Well, like, the whole house is a portable unit. They got these units of glass apartments stacked on top of each other, and I think I was supposed to move out or something, 'cause these choppers come swooping through the trees, and these searchlights come right through the glass walls, and you were tryin' to fix the blinds so the helicopters couldn't see us, and I was gettin' pretty paranoid, too, so we run out into the street and I try to distract them. I unhook the trailer truck that's attached to the stack of apartments, and they start rolling down this hill, and you run into the bushes and then I hear gunshots and I woke up."

"Wow, pretty freaky."

"Yeah, it was weird but kinda fun, y'know, like a movie."

"Un-huh." I looked down at the small stack of rolled joints. I craved another, but knew I was already as stoned as I was going to get. Ed sipped his beer.

"You goin' campin' tonight?" I asked him.

"Naw, Michelle and I are gonna go out."

I was secretly thrilled. My first night alone with Randy. Now, to merely dispense with Shawna. "Whose parents aren't home?" I asked.

"Hers. We're goin' to her place." He smiled.

"Aha." I scooted out of my chair. "And on that pleasant note I shall bid you adieu."

"Adieu and a doobie." He handed me another joint.

"Thank you, kind sir."

"Hey, don' let that dream freak ya out."

"Right."

I grabbed another beer from the fridge and headed back to the porch. Shawna sat alone on the steps, smoking a cigarette. I felt like talking to her seriously, about the stuff her mom was going on about, but we were in a good mood, so I just tried to enjoy myself.

I could have told her right there. I can get quite blunt if I'm drunk enough. I stood for a moment, admiring Shawna's back, her long hair a dozen shades of blonde and brown. She liked me a lot. She was one of my best friends. Why couldn't I just tell her? It shouldn't make any difference. But of course, it did.

It made all the difference in the world.

Randy came out onto the porch with a beer in each hand. "Here they are, our dance team from Minneapolis!"

Shawna turned, surprised. "I didn't even hear you guys!"

"Surprise, surprise!"

I sat down next to her. Randy sat and handed her a beer, pushing himself between me and Shawna. Our thighs touched, just like in choir. He wrapped his arms around both of us. Whenever he did things like that, I loved him but felt so confused.

"The East German judge gave you a 9.8." Randy said into my ear.

"And the Russian judge?" Shawna asked.

"Nyet! Nyet!" Randy shouted.

I gulped down more beer.

"Well, my children," Randy said. "It seems that our dear Edward has departed with a party member of the opposite sex."

"Michelle?" I asked.

"Michelle?" Shawna jokingly repeated.

"Michelle," Randy admitted with Walter Cronkite authority.

"The dirty traitor," I brooded. Shawna giggled and nearly choked on a sip of beer.

"Ha!" I jumped up. "The slatternly woman! Only the gods can save her now!" I stood back in the middle of the yard. "JEEE-ZUSS! Hep this poh misguided creachah in heh owah of NEED!" I stiffened as if hit by a bolt of divine lightning and fell back on the lawn into a pile of leaves.

After some more joking we finished our beers and headed inside. Melanie was still standing with her friends. I talked some more with her and asked her to the dance next Saturday and of course she said yes. Big thrill. I acted like I was surprised and thrilled and she had just made me so happy. I'm very good at doing fake polite things when I have to.

Shawna stayed at the party, saying she'd get a ride home from one of her friends. Randy and I left in his old Mustang. We'd already packed our camping stuff in the trunk. Randy charmed a six-pack from Jack Adler. Chuck seemed like a lost cause. But being alone with a drunk and stoned Randy still had potential.

11. Biophilia

We drove out to Route 260 and parked on a little dirt road off of Reggie Arnold's farm. Reggie was Randy's father's cousin. He lived all by himself in a little rickety house that smelled like an armpit. Reggie was kind of strange, didn't go into town much. He mostly hunted in the woods near his farm, where he built the little cabin that Randy and I and Ed camped in. Even though it was October, it was cold. We walked about two acres into a stretch of woods, passing under a few fences and by a little pond where we'd gone swimming in the summer.

We got to the cabin and Randy lit the Coleman lantern he'd brought. Inside, the cabin looked exactly as we'd left it from our last visit. A big barrel stove sat against the center of the wall opposite the door. A rickety pipe led up to the ceiling and out the roof. Two musty mattresses lay on the wooden floor. Randy had made a lot of jokes about the wild times he'd had in the cabin. The mattresses made me wonder what kind.

Randy unpacked while I hunted around for some firewood. The

woods around the cabin were dark and calm. I knew there was a small ravine just a few yards in front of the cabin, so I walked around back to make sure I wouldn't fall in. The hum of trucks out on the highway was the only sound that crept into the woods.

When I got back in the cabin, Randy had fixed everything up and laid our sleeping bags side by side on the floor next to the barrel stove. I chucked some of the wood into the fire, and lay the rest to the side.

"Well, what's the surprise?" I asked Randy as I sat on my sleeping bag. I was trying to be cool while I was actually getting all lumpy inside, hoping I could work up the guts to tell him how I felt.

"What surprise?" Randy asked, eyes innocent. The flames lit him warmly, making his hair more golden than I'd ever seen it.

"You know, every time we come out here you got a surprise. The bow and arrow. Last time you taught me how to shoot your rifle."

"Yeah, an' you nearly killed us all."

"Yeah, an' I had a bruise on my shoulder for a week from that damn gun. So, what's the surprise?"

A branch crackled in the barrel stove.

"No big surprise..." Randy pulled a rolled-up plastic bag out of the pocket of his down jacket. "...except a bit of hash."

"Juicy!" I yelled. Getting stoned in the woods with Randy; perfect, I thought.

He laid out the bits and pieces of hallucinogenic stuff on his sleeping bag. "Now, we shouldn't do it all at once. Just a little to test it out and then more to fly on."

"Mmmm, a man who knows his drugs."

"A waste is a terrible thing to mind."

We sipped beers carefully and ingested the precious hash, lighting it on a pin and sucking up the smoke that he collected under a cup.

"Ah," Randy leaned back, admiring the flames. "A good fire, a good buzz, and a good friend."

My heart thumped.

"Man, I'm flyin' on this," I said after the hash began to set in. "Man, I can feel all the years of work put into this little bit of dried stuff that lays in my belly. I can feel the brown callused fingers of the little South Americans plucking this stuff and the deep dark dirt that it got plucked out of. I can feel the warm mountain sun baking the backs of little children playing in the fields and their giggling little black marble eyes."

Randy looked at me admiringly.

"The flavors in the air here are so great!" I got up and yelled out the door. "FUCKIN' GREAT!!!" I rolled down to the floor, a little closer to Randy. He didn't seem to mind.

"Man, the dirt in this place, the wood, the wood smell...musta been great when you first used this place."

"Yeah," Randy nodded. "Some pretty wild times back then."

"Like what?"

"Gettin' drunk, messin' around, y' know."

"Like what? What'd you do with Cliff and those guys?" Randy used to hang around with Cliff Spierman and a bunch of other guys that had graduated. In a way, we had that much in common, never making good friends with guys our own age, preferring older, more experienced friends and younger ones to share those experiences.

"You know, jus' the usual stuff."

"Like what?"

"Stupid stuff. Pissin' contests, circle jerks." He smiled.

"I don't believe it."

"Then don't."

"You messed around with other guys?"

"It was nothin'."

"J'ever do anything else like that?" I was trying to be cool but I think the hash made me feel reckless. What the hell.

"A few times."

I looked at Randy. The flames danced in his eyes.

"Would you ever do it again?" I asked.

Randy shrugged.

"C'mere," I said I leaned close to him and kissed him lightly on the lips. My head thumped and the ringing in my ears made me giddy.

He didn't resist, didn't hit me, didn't shove me away. We looked each other in the eyes. I kissed him again, deeper. His lips and tongue and teeth were warm and wet, so inviting with all the hard wood smells around. I reached around and put my arm around Randy's waist, but he pulled back. I still had the taste of him in my mouth when I saw the disappointment in his eyes.

"You shouldn't do that," he said softly.

"Why not?" I wanted to say I loved him, but my throat choked up.

"Let's be friends, okay? I know you're... always have, but let's just be friends."

He put his hand on my shoulder. I could have just said okay and then tried to get over it, but I have a way of messing things up. I stood up and walked to the door, shoving my hands into the pockets of my down coat.

"Just be friends? Just be your little buddy, right? Just keep on pretending that...." I choked up and kicked a beer can. "I just..." I pleaded with him, but the words got caught up in my throat, fighting with tears to get out.

"You know, I gave up on a chance with someone else. Someone..."

I stormed out and started off through the black woods.

"Tom!" Randy yelled out. "Dammit, Tom!"

I wanted to turn right around and give him a big hug and be friends again, or instead punch him, but the something in me that likes to mess things up just kept walking. I tripped over branches and fell into puddles of half-frozen mud and bog. I got to the light of the farmhouse and went down the dirt road to the highway.

I walked, hoping some truck would swerve over and run me down since I was too chicken to run out in the road. My hands got cold. My face was teary and snotty. I kept wiping it on the puffy sleeve of my coat, but it didn't do much good.

I got to the last hill before the road led down into town and stopped. Except for the repeating roar of trucks and cars, the whole horizon was silent. Plainfield glowed from the cluster of streetlights.

I almost got to the point of calming down, of accepting things, and feeling better, but then I pictured Randy's beautiful face pulling away from me. I let out an angry scream and kept screaming until something cracked in my throat. I listened to the echo, expecting someone to talk back or lightning to strike, but all I got back was the wheezing silence of that hill, dark and humped, like the tired ghost of an old Indian waiting for me to get off his back and grow up.

After a while more of walking, I saw the headlights approach behind me, then Randy's Mustang to pulled up beside me.

He reached over and rolled down the window. "Come on, sport."

"Fuck you."

"That's not on the menu."

I shook my head. "Son of a bitch."

"Forget the camping. I got your stuff. Let's get you home for some shut-eye before that speech team thing."

"Oh, yeah, another trophy."

I opened the door, slumped inside, rolled up the window as he drove on.

"Maybe more than that."

12. Symbiosis

I never thought of Randy as prescient; wise beyond his years, perhaps. But in a half hour, I would slump into bed after rousing my father despite tiptoeing upstairs.

In four hours, I would settle into Mrs. Schafer's station wagon after calling her to say that I would be going to the tournament in New Philly. The three of my other teammates who rode along had heard the gossip about my fight and begged for details. I ignored them, still queasy from a slight hangover and a trace of the pot and hash buzz.

I sat in the front, Mrs. Schafer giving me some serious side eye. "Well, we're glad to have you along." She didn't ask why I hadn't stayed camping.

After the shuffle of registering and getting our classroom assignments, I wished Tara good luck before she went to the library with the other debate kids to research their sources for the topic of the season, 'U.S. intervention in overseas combat.'

I saw Chuck standing outside our first assigned classroom.

Although I'd answered it many times, with various made-up answers, Chuck's stunned look and his sincere, "What happened?" made me unspool the truth, and a few of the funnier details.

"Aw, my poor buddy!"

He grabbed me in a close hug, a long, very close hug. I felt warm tingles up and down my body, and for a moment our hips brushed a bit too close. Yup, boners bumped.

"Where were you last week?" I kept a close grip, maybe too close.

"Oh, I was hungover."

"Pffft. Lame excuse. I'm hungover now."

Chuck pulled back, blushing, stole a glance downward, adjusted himself, and whispered, "After second round, before the awards. You and me."

I knew what he meant. Unless he was trying to psyche me out, he wanted some alone time. But where?

"But first…" He finished adjusting his pants. "We find some coffee."

For the next two hours, Chuck and I would sneak glances at each other through three rounds of classroom competition, his main f ocal point being me, and mine him.

Once again, my competitors went through their predictable essays and play excerpts. Freddy was once again point-perfect. Chuck sat at the desk beside me, and I could almost feel his body heat as he stole furtive glances in my direction.

I was called before him, and managed to keep calm, since my short story was pretty well rehearsed. And I'd focused instead on the wall behind him, instead of looking at him, because he was just smiling at me with such a clever grin.

But somewhere in the middle of his Tennessee Williams tale, he fumbled, it seemed, and lost his place, but then recovered. I noticed the teacher/judge make a note.

Moments after that round was completed, and we were dismissed, he led me down a hallway that hadn't been used for competition. After peeking into a few doors, he snuck me off into a darkened science room at the end of the hall. We both knew that the debaters took longer, and the judges would discuss who should win for another half hour.

Chuck took me by the hand, leading me to a corner desk out of view of the door's window.

"My little warrior," he muttered. "Lemme kiss your booboo."

A light peck on my forehead, then my nose, then my lips, which parted, maybe too soon, maybe not, because our tongues started slipping around, our hands reaching for hips, butts, anything.

As we embraced, I felt I noticed him fumbling with his pants, guiding my hand downward. He smelled of aftershave, coffee and something else; I couldn't place it, something earthy and warm.

I heard two kids walking by chattering away far down the hall outside, and pulled back.

"Wait. Did you flub your reading on purpose?"

"For you? No. I like you, but–"

"But–"

"I was just so worked up knowing this was next." Chuck pulled me close, kissed me again as he unzipped his pants.

"What if we miss the awards?" I whispered.

"Oh, Freddy can take all the trophies. You got your prize right here."

It was difficult to argue with his boner jutting out of his fly and thrust into my hand.

He pressed closer, kissing me again. He groaned into my mouth, and everything else melted away. Trophies, Briggs, Randy, Mr. Rick's corduroy pants, everything dissolved into scattered mist with every thud of my heart.

Instead, I foresaw us alternating first, second and third place for the rest of the season, sometimes losing to Freddy and his near-perfect James Baldwin speech, but not caring.

Imagining schemes at the state tournament for us to share a

hotel room alone flew around my mind. I saw the days and months of Chuck and I driving to each other's homes on later weekends, our parents perhaps suspecting more than a friendship, but not interfering.

In my mind, I saw all of our future awkward, hilarious attempts to be alone; county roads, abandoned parking lots, under the bleachers of a darkened stadium.

He guided my head down to his waist where I attempted to offer my own oral interpretation. For a moment, as he shoved himself into me, and as I almost choked, I even saw a flash-forward with some heartache, missing each other, breaking dates, almost breaking up, tearful reunions, college choices, where we might live together, and a flurry of unanswered questions.

As we traded places, Chuck knelt before me, undoing my belt, zipper and pants, clutching my hips as his mouth bobbed below me, my tie slung over my neck, my pants undone. He hummed and giggled for a moment when he took a momentary break, then resumed with a hurried fervor.

Gripping the edge of the cold black lab table with one hand, gently petting his head with the other, I gazed up at the colorful posters above the green chalkboard and relaxed, comforted by the natural beauty: Kingdom, Phylum, Class, Order, Family, Genus, Species.

Jim Provenzano is the author of *Finding Tulsa* (Palm Drive Publishing), *Now I'm Here* (Beautiful Dreamer Press), the Lambda Literary Award-winning *Every Time I Think of You*, its sequel *Message of Love* (a Lambda Literary Award Finalist), the novels *PINS*, *Monkey Suits*, *Cyclizen*, the commissioned stage adaptation of *PINS*, and the short story collection *Forty Wild Crushes*. Audiobook adaptations include *PINS* (Paul Fleschner, narrator), *Every Time I Think of You*, and its sequel *Message of Love* (Michael Wetherbee, narrator).

Born in New York City and raised in Ashland, Ohio, he studied theatre at Kent State University, has a BFA in Dance from Ohio State University and a Master of Arts in English/Creative Writing from San Francisco State University. A journalist, editor, and photographer in LGBT media for more than three decades, he lives in San Francisco.

www.jimprovenzano.com
www.jimprovenzano.blogspot.com
www.twitter.com/jim_provenzano
www.threads.net/@jimprovenzano
www.facebook.com/JimProvenzanoAuthor
www.youtube.com/@Cyclizen
www.amazon.com/Jim-Provenzano/e/B000APM4MW
www.goodreads.com/author/show/620500.Jim_Provenzano

Praise for Jim Provenzano's other books

Finding Tulsa (Palm Drive Publishing)

"It's not easy writing a novel in the first person and relying on the sole perspective of your narrator, but Jim Provenzano pulls it off beautifully in *Finding Tulsa*. He brings us the remarkable voice and life experience of Stan Grozniak, a struggling Hollywood director and a nuanced gay man in a town where so many live on the surface of things... *Finding Tulsa* is both a unique and satisfying read that gives much perspective on the AIDS pandemic and living through it as a modern gay man."
– *Art & Understanding*

"Written as an autobiography, this entertaining work of fiction tells the story of Stan, a gay film director making a film about his past. Cast in the movie is Lance, a boyhood crush who Stan reconnects with in Hollywood. *Finding Tulsa* is an intense story, yet it's an easy read due to the author's vivid writing."
– *Echo Magazine*

"*Finding Tulsa* is more than just the pseudo-memoir of a Hollywood hotshot and his sexual escapades (however exciting they are to read about – and in lurid, delicious detail), but also an unexpected, endearing love story. ... Whether it's a smalltown production of *Gypsy* or a porno movie set in the desert, Stan's limitless passion for creativity and the artistic process remains intact, and guides him throughout."
– *Edge Media Network*

"*Finding Tulsa* is a smashing exploration of what it would be like to be a gay film director of some renown living his best life. Mostly, I loved how recognizably messy Stan is, yet still makes his life work, which, for Stan, includes finding love with his unrequited high school crush and making a living through film; an excellent read for anyone who is interested in complex, first-person narratives."
– *Joyfully Jay*

"*Finding Tulsa* reminds you what a good friend a novel can be. It's about friendship, about "losing men and then finding them," about brotherly love and conflict, and the possibility of resolution. It's sexy, funny, astute, panoramic – it knows about suburban Ohio basement rec rooms and glam parties in the Hollywood hills. I felt like I had met a charming guy at a cocktail party who seemed to get me, understood my past, confided his own, and then disappeared to another better party before I was ready for him to leave. And it's wrapped around a fearless, wrenching narrative about facing your childhood demons, raising the question of whether or not one of the demons might have been you. There's so much to savor, to argue with, reflect upon, learn from, enjoy."
– John Weir, author of *The Irreversible Decline of Eddie Socket*

"*Finding Tulsa* is sexy, romantic, witty, engaging, both cleverly current yet sweetly retrospective. It's Jim Provenzano's most complex and accomplished novel. He gets so much right and so evocatively about show business, from those school plays we all remember to Hollywood made-for-television movies, with delicious stops at boyhood Super-8 movies and out of town gay porn shoots."
– Felice Picano, author of the *New York Times* best-seller *Like People in History*

"Everything's coming up roses in *Finding Tulsa*, Jim Provenzano's intoxicating portrait of an artist as young to middle-aged man, from a high school musical techie in torn shorts to a semi jaded independent gay filmmaker. It's a well-told yarn, full of humor and panache about a Hollywood player torn between his boyhood crush and a porn star. Spin the bottle, ride the Rolodex, and fasten your seat belt for Provenzano's sweet roller coaster ride."
– Marc Huestis, film director (*Sex Is* ...) and author of *Impresario of Castro Street: an Intimate Showbiz Memoir*

"Jim Provenzano must have been spying on me from my adolescence (making short films with my brother) to my adulthood (making gay movies and TV series). I identified with every twist, turn, and blow by blow of this sexy show biz saga!"
– Sam Irvin, Director of *Dante's Cove*, Co-Producer of *Gods and Monsters* and *The Broken Hearts Club*

"Lights! Camera! Action! *Finding Tulsa* is a show-biz comedy told by a witty industry insider divulging how plays and movies and characters like 'Tulsa' help gay boys survive adolescence, create identity, and worship beauty. What better icons could Provenzano have picked than Sondheim and *Gypsy* on which to fly his vivid characters, backstage intrigues, and dialogue sure to thrill the theater and movie queen in all of us. Writing at the top of his powers, with his striped tie and hopes high, he's got rhythm. All he needs is you to go with 'im. A splendid romp! Let him entertain you!"
– Jack Fritscher, author of *Some Dance to Remember*

"Jim Provenzano's sexy, funny and soulful novel *Finding Tulsa* is a beautiful deep-end dive into the memory of desire, the thumping bass note that drives life and art. The novel gorgeously explores how our hearts and cocks are woven with our theatre and films as we figure out how to be the star of our own queer story."
– Tim Miller, Performer and author of *A Body in the O*

"Jim Provenzano always keeps in mind what the original 'Tulsa' said in *Gypsy*: 'This step is good for the costume.' Provenzano never misses a step as he suavely combines aesthetics and homoerotics in a work that is throughout deeply touching."
– David Ehrenstein, author of *Open Secret: Gay Hollywood–1928-2000*

Now I'm Here (Beautiful Dreamer Press)

"In *Now I'm Here*, a Queen show serves as backdrop to a burgeoning romance. In addition to conveying the power of listening to music, Provenzano captures the intensity of making it: When Joshua, a piano prodigy and would-be rock star, sets fingers to keyboard, Provenzano beautifully renders his passionate character's combination of fugue state and frenzy."
– *San Francisco Examiner*

"This storytelling method effectively and passionately conveys the lengthy, turbulent evolution of their compelling, inspiring and uplifting relationship... The love story of Joshua and David reminds the reader how to appreciate the extraordinary in the ordinary. Professionally speaking, neither of these men achieves fame or accomplishes anything especially newsworthy, but what they share emotionally is nothing short of remarkable. Some books you read for laughter, intrigue, debate or information. *Now I'm Here* makes you feel."
– *Edge Media Network*

"California author Jim Provenzano joins the great novelists who have written important and lasting novels about men in love, and while he has won prizes for his work it is now, with his publication of *Now I'm Here* that he joins the ranks of the major authors who have had a lasting imprint on our society and the LGBTIQ community. André Aciman, Andrew Holleran, Colm Toibin, Edmund White, and now Jim Provenzano are important artists whose impact is significant."
– *San Francisco Review of Books*

"Provenzano reminds us of a swath of gay men and boys who remain largely overlooked; the small town, Midwestern gays whose psyches, like their turf, have been regarded as flyover country. As Provenzano traces the friendship and falling outs between Eric and his two closest friends through the 1970s and 1980s, we hear untold tales of sexual awakening among the decidedly un-'woke,' we see the long- nailed finger of HIV/AIDS scratching far beyond big cities, and we are reminded how limited our sense of 'gay community' can sometimes be."
– *Passport*

"Provenzano has honed his craft and takes you on this dizzying ride with the able assurance of a pro. His rendering of the mid-Seventies is deadly accurate ... and will bring a smile of remembrance to your face if you were coming of age then. He never miss-steps or falls short of the mark emotionally, either. The characters are all organic, built and embroidered on with well-chosen detail, and this never once feels false or contrived as many romances do. So, even if you're not exactly a Queen fan (and why not, I wonder?), you'll enjoy this supremely well-plotted and populated romance. Highly recommended."
– *Out in Print*

"Joshua and David come to life through Provenzano's prose, as does the town of Serene. The story beautifully conveys the exhilaration of love, the power of music, and the profound sadness of loss. The late '70s and '80s were the last remnants of a more innocent time. Provenzano's deft writing whisks readers back to those halcyon days."
– *Prizm News*

"Set in a fictional Ohio town like the one Provenzano grew up in himself, *Now I'm Here* is the story of Joshua and David, two teenagers who fall in love in 1978. Their passionate affair grows into a life together in the face of religious intolerance, 'rehabilitation therapy,' and perhaps most significantly, the heartbreak of AIDS."
– *Los Angeles Blade*

Message of Love (Lambda Literary Award finalist, 2015)

"The sequel to the Lambda Literary Award-winning *Every Time I Think of You* reintroduces readers to Everett and Reid as they traverse the next phases of their relationship. It is 1980 Philadelphia, and the couple has settled into their first year at Temple University, together exploring the city and campus and adjusting to dormitory domesticity. *Message of Love* is a brilliant retelling of young love and the transformations it undergoes as lovers grow from adolescence to adulthood."
– *Philadelphia Gay News*

"*Message of Love* is an earnest, heartfelt and refreshing continuation of a young couple's adventures that leaves the reader excited, amused and inspired."
– *Edge Media*

"I loved the way they interacted and wove themselves so completely into each other's lives. The way it was written was pure genius on Provenzano's part. I'll say it again: his writing is gorgeous and sweeping and strong."
– *Boys in Our Books*

"The richness of its details and the complexities of its characters will make this a story to remember. If you are new to Reid and Everett's story, then begin with *Every Time I Think of You*. If you are familiar with that novel, then *Message of Love* is a story not to be missed, a wonderfully satisfying and uplifting novel, certainly one of the best of 2014."
– *Scattered Thoughts & Rogue Words*

"A vivid and accurate depiction of a moment in time and history, *Message of Love* is an honest and unsentimental portrayal of the difficulties of sustaining even the strongest relationship and is, ultimately, an inspiring validation of the power of commitment."
– Tom Mendicino, author of *Probation* and *KC, at Bat*

"Sexy and uninhibitedly queer. As a bisexual person with a disability and especially as a wheelchair user, I found the story to be written in a refreshing and honest tone without falling prey to the pity approach as it relates to loving somebody with a disability. Jim Provenzano's *Message of Love* successfully represents positive crip and queer sexuality. Bravo!"
– Maria R. Palacios, author of *The Female King* and
Criptionary-Disability Humor and Satire

Every Time I Think of You
(Lambda Literary Award winner, 2012)

"Their love is a force of nature ... Provenzano's sweet humor throughout the book is what makes it such a moving and satisfying read. While he certainly brings the reader to a deeper understanding of being differently-abled, he never resorts to preaching his message. These boys are too real for that."
– *Lambda Literary Review*

"A sense of youthful, romantic optimism ... permeates the novel as a whole."
– Erika Jahneke, *Breath and Shadow*

"*Every Time I Think of You* opens readers' eyes, minds and hearts to corners of the world they may never have realized existed. Everett's paralysis is less metaphoric, more an opportunity to explore the effect of disability on two growing boys who just happen to be gay. It's not easy to write a novel about sports, gay teenagers and sex in (and out of) wheelchairs. Jim Provenzano has done it, with grace and power."
– Dan Woog, syndicated columnist, 'The Outfield'

"With Reid and Everett, the author has created two counterparts that complement each other beautifully. Their romance, simple and pure, yet heated and passionate, is strikingly genuine. Furthermore, they're both likable, so much so that the reader can't help but cheer for them. Even the most jaded among us will experience a renewed faith in love and romance after reading it."
–*Edge Media*

"A beautiful story of friendship, devotion and love, as well as a practical lesson on dealing with physically challenged individuals."
–*Echo Magazine*

"Sweet, and tender, with the right feeling for a teenage love story."
– *Elisa Reviews*

"Provenzano's characters are rich and complex. His sense of pace and plotting are dead on, so things never drag, and his prose is straightforward and never showy. It's a well-told tale whose aim to inform as well as entertain certainly hits the mark."
– *Out in Print*

"There are so many levels of nuance to Provenzano's story. Reading about the clever ways in which they find to spend time together is inspiring and touching. It's an exciting voyage of discovery, for them and for readers alike. When the story takes its more serious turn, *Every Time I Think of You* becomes a tale of heartbreak, courage, and healing. It's a remarkable, uplifting story."
– *Windy City Times*

Cyclizen

"From the ashes of office temp arises a courier on two wheels in search of the man who got away. As he whizzes up and down the thoroughfares of Manhattan, fleeing his past, sizing up his future, he careens headlong into lust's pothole. Watch our hero as he falls under the spell of a dashing and dastardly inside trader. How far will the seduction go? Only the Cyclizen knows."
– Ian Philips, author of *See Dick Deconstruct*

"Juggling AIDS activism, corporate and individual greed, all through the travails of a bike messenger in search of love and belonging, *Cyclizen* is noteworthy for its fine characterization and poignant lyricism. Provenzano explores love and friendship with insight and nuance, marking his work as unique, vital and significant."
– Trebor Healey, author of *Through It Came Bright Colors*

Monkey Suits

"Jim Provenzano's brilliant novel *Monkey Suits* captures perfectly the Reagan Age as it examines the lives of gay cater-waiters working the Metropolitan Museum's swank parties while getting politicized."
– *Bay Area Reporter*

"A nostalgic mix of sex and melodrama, *Monkey Suits* is a fun read, jammed with in-jokes, intrigue and involving characters. It's those details and finishing touches that make the book a sultry page-turner. Better than most gay novels, and infinitely better dressed."
– *Torso Magazine*

"A wit that equals Maupin at his best, using the figure of the cater waiter as his Everyman... A thoroughly entertaining and well-written story filled with well-defined characters, clever plot twists and subtle humor... light-handed irony and a sharp eye for dark humor around the edges."
– *Independent Writers Forum*

"A nostalgic Manhattan-set novel about unfocused youth, mercurial boyfriends, and the early days of activism and anger. Part sneering and part servile, a nervy imbalance gives this novel a subversive, comic clout."
– Richard LaBonté, *Bookmarks*

PINS (Myrmidude Press)

"What starts off as yet another coming-of-age tale of gay youth in suburbia takes a dramatic turn and careens into a full-fledged miracle of writing. *PINS* seduces the reader into thinking that sex is the only thing on its mind. By the time Provenzano is through with his story, however, some universal truths have been examined and harshly displayed."
— *New York Blade*

"A brooding chronicle of Catholic guilt, faith, family and sexuality in a New Jersey of intolerance. The characters here are real and loaded with depth, making the action and uncertain ending that much more vivid and ultimately poignant. *PINS* is an auspicious debut, sort of a *Catcher in the Rye* about disillusioned gay jocks. It firmly establishes Jim Provenzano as an important new voice in early 21st-century fiction."
— *Torso Magazine*

"Fully captures the reader ... a descriptive writer of the Ernest Hemingway model; terse, stripped down, and to the point."
— *Lambda Book Report*

"Provenzano has a swift and flexible style that cuts against sentiment and reveals, in moments of grace, something like true feeling. He's also funny. He has an ear for teenage banter, and he's tartly lyrical about Jersey towns, Italian families and homemade mix tapes with titles like GRAPPLE and AURGH. Most urgent, he shows how gay bashing is still an outlet for kids who grew up in the so-called gay '90s."
— *The Advocate*

"The author brings evident personal knowledge and a crisp, uncluttered prose style to this coming-out saga."
— *East Bay Express*

"A brilliant piece of fiction… The plot is very complex with many layers, each well-developed and passionately expressed. No sensitive reader will make it to the end without giggling, anxiety, joy and tears."
— *Gay People's Chronicle*

Printed in the USA
CPSIA information can be obtained
at www.ICGtesting.com
LVHW030600150524
780221LV00013B/788